CAROLINA PRIDE

This Large Print Book carries the
Seal of Approval of N.A.V.H.

NORTH CAROLINA, BOOK ONE

CAROLINA PRIDE

A NOVEL OF ROMANCE NESTLED IN THE HEART OF THE TAR HEEL STATE

TERRY FOWLER

THORNDIKE PRESS

An imprint of Thomson Gale, a part of The Thomson Corporation

Detroit • New York • San Francisco • New Haven, Conn. • Waterville, Maine • London

LIBRARY OF CONGRESS CATALOGING-IN-PUBLICATION DATA

Fowler, Terry (Terry S.)
  Carolina pride : a novel of romance nestled in the heart of the Tar Heel State / by Terry Fowler.
     p. cm. — (North Carolina ; bk. 1)
  ISBN-13: 978-0-7862-9479-4 (hardcover : alk. paper)
  ISBN-10: 0-7862-9479-5 (hardcover : alk. paper)
  1. Lawyers — Fiction. 2. Farm life — Fiction. 3. North Carolina — Fiction. 4. Large type books I. Title.
PS3556.O86C37 2007
813'.54—dc22   2007000692

Published in 2007 by arrangement with Barbour Publishing, Inc.

Printed in the United States of America on permanent paper
10 9 8 7 6 5 4 3 2 1

Dear Reader,

I love calling North Carolina home. For me, *A Sense of Belonging, Carolina Pride,* and *Look to the Heart* reflect the heart and soul of North Carolina — home and family.

Always an avid reader, I dreamed of becoming a librarian, but circumstances prevailed and I work full time in an office.

After losing my parents in 1991 and having my own medical crises in 1992, I accepted I couldn't do it alone. I gave my life to God.

God had plans to use my love of books in a different way. My greatest joy is to witness for my beloved Savior in my writing.

I'm the second oldest in a family of five and share a home with my sister. She's also my best friend. I also enjoy working in my church, gardening, home decorating, and genealogical research. Please visit my webpage at www.terryfowler.net.

Yours in Christ,
Terry Fowler

CHAPTER 1

Okay, God, here's another fine mess I've gotten myself into. Liza Stephens stood defeated in the latest battle of her life — that of a seventy-pound puppy and a five-pound cat. Listening to them growl and hiss at each other throughout the ten-mile drive should have clued her in that she was heading for trouble. Instead, she'd ignored the situation.

After parking at the vet's office, she'd grabbed Barney, her Saint Bernard puppy, under one arm and Fluff, her mother's cat, under the other. It was then that Barney took offense to Fluff's presence, and his fight to reach the cat resulted in Liza's current dilemma.

Mama always said God looked out for fools and children. Right now, Liza certainly felt she belonged in the first category. Why did doing good deeds always seem to backfire on her?

Liza eyed her purse on the roof of the car, just out of reach. She could let go of either of the animals to retrieve it, but Barney was an obedience school dropout; Liza doubted her mother would appreciate her allowing Fluff to take off for the woods, probably with Barney hot on her trail.

It wouldn't work anyway. Her oversized shirt was caught in the car door, effectively pinning her to the side of the car. Liza leaned back to wait. Hopefully someone would soon leave the vet's office, and she could further embarrass herself by asking for help.

"Stop it, Barney," she snapped when the dog made a move for Fluff. She tried shifting the cat away, only to be jerked back by her shirttail. She was well and truly stuck.

Dropping the keys into her bag probably hadn't been the smartest thing she'd ever done. A new thought entered her head. What if a thief took advantage of her predicament?

Leave it to her — and all because she tried to be a good daughter. It wasn't enough to spend half the night working with her dad on his books. Her mother shook her awake at the crack of dawn on a Saturday morning with a request to take Barney and Fluff to the vet.

"Not together," she objected. "They'll kill each other."

"I'll ask your dad to do it later."

"No. I'll take them."

After all, Barney was her pet. Maybe she should just let him go for help. Another bad idea. He definitely did not understand the premise of being a rescue animal. Letting go of Barney would probably mean neither she nor Fluff would survive. She was already caught between the two of them. There was no need to get teeth and claws involved.

"You'd think you two could get along after six months," she muttered.

Barney's response was a low growl in his throat and a renewed fight for freedom.

"Shut up, idiot."

"Excuse me?"

Liza looked straight into the eyes of the most handsome man she'd seen in a long time. He stood tall and confident, his hair a sun-streaked brown, his face a mixture of jutting cheekbones, strong nose, arrogant chin, and the most penetrating blue eyes she'd ever encountered.

"No. No . . . not you," Liza stammered. "The dog. I seem to have gotten myself into a predicament." Shifting the animals, she said, "My shirt's caught in the car door."

He chuckled, and Liza felt a telltale blush

trailing its way over her face. She hated situations like this — feeling out of control. "Could you get my keys? They're in my bag."

He lifted the purse and flipped the flap back, glancing at her. "May I?"

"Please do."

Watching him remove item after item, Liza grew even more embarrassed. One of these days, she was going to clean that thing out. She'd put it on her schedule, right after the next time she took these two animals anywhere ever again.

She released a relieved sigh at the welcome jingle of her key ring. The audible click of the locks disengaging when he hit the remote button was a beautiful sound. She tried to shift to open the door and grimaced when the shirt jerked her back again.

"Maybe I should open it from inside."

He went around to the passenger side, and seconds later when the door popped open, she was freed. "Thank You, God," Liza murmured.

He came back around the car and asked, "How did you manage that?"

Everything had happened so fast. While struggling to keep the animals separated, she'd backed up against the door to close it, planning to grab her purse. "It seemed awfully easy at the time. I can't tell you how much I appreciate your help. I figured I'd be caught in the midst of a fur fight any moment."

He chuckled again and held out his hand. "Hi. I'm Lee Hayden."

Liza glanced at the animals and shrugged, lifting Fluff higher to extend her little finger. "Liza Stephens."

Lee grinned and shook her pinkie. "Why don't I lock up the car and help you get your furry friends inside?"

"Thanks again."

"No problem." He pushed the items back into her purse, along with her keys. He tucked it under his arm. "Lead the way."

Lee pulled open the office door and waited for her to go first. She stopped at the chest-high desk and stared at the clipboard. "Hi, Sheila. Could you sign us in?"

"Liza, my goodness. You look great."

"Thanks," she murmured self-consciously. "Barney and Fluff need their shots."

"Have a seat. We'll be with you soon."

Two other Saturday-morning patients waited with their owners in the small waiting area. Liza chose a chair in the corner and sat. Another dilemma arose when she tried to figure out a way to free her hold on the animals. She glanced up as her rescuer spoke to Sheila.

"Could you tell Dr. Wilson that Legrande Hayden is here to see him, please? It's a personal call."

"Certainly, sir. Have a seat."

Lee took the chair next to Liza. "Does he bite?" he asked, indicating Barney.

"He never has before, but today I make no promises."

"I'll hold onto him if you'd like."

"No, I couldn't," Liza said.

"It's no problem."

She considered her dilemma and relented. "If you're sure you don't mind. Just put him on the floor. You don't want dog hair all over your clothes."

Lee shifted Barney to sit by his leg and petted his head. "He's a big fellow."

"He's going to get bigger. Daddy says he doesn't know who eats more — Barney or my horse."

"Unless it's a very small pony, I'd say the horse." The phone rang, and when Sheila answered, Lee glanced at her and back at Liza. "Why did she act so surprised just now?"

Startled by his question, Liza's head jerked up. Leaning back in the yellow plastic chair, she hugged Fluff closer and rubbed a hand over the tabby fur. "My metamorphosis. You could say they knew me when."

"When what?" he persisted.

People's reaction to her changed outer appearance had been startling. Inwardly she was the same, but they rarely looked that deep. "I've lost weight. My changed exterior shocks people." Liza rubbed her neck self-consciously at his intent examination.

"I'm intrigued."

Eager to change the subject, she said, "You've got an interesting name. Legrande. I've never heard it before."

"Lee, please. I try not to use Legrande any more than necessary. I was named after my father and grandfather."

She nodded, a smile touching the corners of her mouth. "Family name. I can identify with that. I'm a heaven-only-knows-what-generation Sarah Elizabeth. The name has been given to the oldest daughter of the oldest daughter in my mother's family for years. I have a grandmother named Elizabeth, a mother named Sarah, and until recently I had a great-grandmother named Beth."

"And you're Liza." Her name slipped easily from his tongue.

Another pet and owner came through the door. After signing in, the man chose a seat farther away from them. The boxer promptly obeyed his command to sit.

"Be quiet," Liza demanded when Barney growled in his throat.

Lee grinned. "He's a brave fellow."

"Not sure if he's brave or stupid. That dog could eat him for lunch. Barney, stop it," she repeated, pulling the dog's head toward her. "You're going to start a fight."

Disdain marked the boxer's owner's face as he looked at Barney. "You need to show that animal who's boss."

"He's just a puppy," Liza defended.

"Who will grow into an unmanageable dog unless you gain control now."

Liza hid her grin in Fluff's fur when the boxer growled at Barney. The man's stern command quieted the animal, but the danger of the situation made her a bit nervous. Maybe she should take Barney out until it was time for the vet to see them.

Sheila noticed the commotion. "Bring them on back, Liza."

Only then did it occur to Liza that she hadn't thought to bring a leash. Seeing her dilemma, Lee caught hold of Barney's collar. "I've got him."

"No, you've done so much already," she protested.

The boxer's owner spoke sharply to his dog when he responded to Barney's growl.

Feeling totally out of her depth, Liza said, "I suppose you think I'm an irresponsible pet owner, too?"

Lee walked between the Saint Bernard and the other dog, pulling up tighter on Barney's collar when he attempted to free himself.

"Dr. Wilson will see you now, sir."

"Actually I think you're the perfect pet owner. It's been my pleasure, Liza."

Lee lifted Barney onto the table in the exam room and said good-bye before following the assistant out into the hallway.

The men's affectionate greeting made Liza wonder about their connection. Fluff jerked her attention back to the animals when Barney made a dive for her, and the cat buried her claws in Liza's side.

"So this knight in shining armor came to your rescue?" her best friend, Kitty Berenson, prompted.

"He freed me from my prison." Liza propped the phone between her ear and shoulder, then stuck the brush into the polish bottle and slid it over her nail. "I hate to think what he thought when he saw me standing there with my arms full of animals and my shirt caught in the car door."

"Tell me about him," Kitty's cheery voice

demanded.

Liza shared all she knew. "I wonder what he's doing here?"

"How long did you say you were you with this guy?"

"Fifteen, twenty minutes."

"And you didn't get his life history? I'm shocked."

No doubt she was. In that amount of time, Kitty would have discovered everything from Lee's date of birth to his current financial status.

"Not all of us have your ability, Kit."

"It is a gift," she boasted playfully, bursting into laughter.

Liza laughed. "Sheila made a big deal out of my appearance, and he asked why."

"Hmm. I think he's interested. Maybe you'll see him again soon."

"I doubt that."

"Too bad. Sounds like a nice guy. Gotta run. Dave's picking me up soon."

"Don't forget our duet in the morning."

"Why don't you just sing a solo? You sing better anyway."

Liza leaned forward. "Kitty, you promised."

"Okay, don't tie yourself in knots. I'll be there."

Her tense muscles relaxed. "You think

tonight's the night?"

"I don't know what Dave's thinking. I'm sure he'll get around to popping the question one of these days."

"He'd better do it soon if you want that June wedding."

Kitty sighed loudly. "Too late for a June wedding now. I'd never get it planned in time."

"You've been planning this wedding since you were seven. You're going to get married down by the pond."

"Tastes change," Kitty said. "When I say 'I do' to David Evans, it's going to be a wedding this town won't forget anytime soon. Take care."

Liza replaced the phone and leaned back against her pillows, fanning her hands to dry the clear polish. Thoughts of Kitty and Dave's romance were soon replaced with fantasies of finding her own Prince Charming.

Every day she prayed that the Lord would send her life partner soon, but the situation seemed more and more hopeless. Not only was there a shortage of men in their small country town, but those she knew treated her more like their kid sister than an eligible female.

She had to agree with Kit on one matter:

It was too bad Lee Hayden wouldn't be around. She could easily see him in the role of knight.

CHAPTER 2

Struggling to get her key into the lock, Liza juggled her briefcase and the mail, frowning when the old door opened easily. Mr. Wilson must have come in early again. After laying the mail on her desk, she went into the kitchenette to put on the coffee. It had become part of her routine since the day she'd found her boss disastrously close to poisoning himself and their clients with his own unpalatable brew.

While it perked, Liza opened the mail and pulled files, humming the song she and Kit had sung at church the previous day. Sometimes she found it difficult to believe she was actually standing before the congregation and singing.

What a difference the years had made! In high school, she'd suffered from terminal shyness. Even the thought of a simple oral book report caused nightmares. But that was before she figured out the miracles God was capable of when He said, "You can."

Lifting the stack of files, she stopped off to pour coffee in her boss's favorite mug. Liza pushed his office door open and was rendered speechless.

With the exception of a tattered hat sporting fishing lures of all descriptions, the desktop was clear. Her workaholic boss leaned dangerously far back in his chair, his feet propped on the corner of the desk. Clothes that had seen better days replaced his usual conservative suit.

Liza chuckled. "You forget to change this morning?"

His feet dropped to the floor. "Morning, Liza. I just came by to tell you I'm taking your advice and going on vacation and to make the introductions."

Liza set the coffee cup on his desk. "Introductions?" she repeated curiously.

John Wilson sipped the coffee and said, "I couldn't expect you to take on the office single-handedly."

"You could have," Liza mumbled. It wasn't as if she'd be idle. She had cases to research, tons of filing, and a phone that never stopped ringing.

"What was that?" he asked absently, missing her remark when a fluorescent orange lure on the hat caught his attention.

"Nothing." More than a little confused, Liza concentrated on spreading the files across the desktop. John Wilson wasn't usually a spur-of-the-moment man. Why now?

"We have a new attorney joining us."

"New attorney?" Liza parroted. What had changed? Mr. Wilson had always maintained they could do the work of six normal people. Why hadn't he mentioned his plans before?

"Should be arriving anytime now." The tan hat flopped back and forth with his efforts to release the fishhook. "First-class lawyer. Glad to get him," he rambled on. "Feels he needs to get out of Charlotte. Thinks this is a good opportunity to see another side of law."

"Sounds fascinating," Liza muttered.

"I hope I am."

Liza spun about to find Lee Hayden propped against the doorjamb. His look was one of faint amusement; his penetrating gaze fixed on her. "Leave your furry friends home today?"

She'd imagined meeting the handsome stranger again, but not like this. Surely he wasn't the new attorney? Mr. Wilson confirmed her suspicions by moving from behind the desk and hurrying to greet him.

"Glad to have you with us. Any problem locating the office?"

Lee straightened and grasped the man's hand. "None at all. You give excellent directions."

"Good. Good," he said, patting Lee on the shoulder. "Did you find a place to stay? There's always room at the house."

"I'm at the hotel."

Needing time to compose herself, Liza turned to leave.

"Oh yes," Mr. Wilson said, catching her arm when she started past him. "I want to introduce you to my secretary. Elizabeth Stephens, this is my nephew, Legrande Hayden."

His secretary? He hadn't called her that since she'd received her paralegal degree. Sure, she still did the typing and filing, but she was more than clerical help.

"We've met, sir," Liza acknowledged. "He came to my rescue Saturday at Dr. Wilson's office. Nice to see you again, Mr. Hayden. Welcome to the firm."

"Good. Good." Mr. Wilson gathered his hat from the desk, downed the coffee, and handed Liza the cup. "Teach him everything I've taught you. I'll see you both in a couple of weeks."

"But you have appointments," she said, totally baffled by his strange behavior.

"Lee can handle them. Help him."

Mr. Wilson chuckled at her surprised expression, tapping her chin to tip her mouth closed before he walked toward the door. His cheerful whistle filled the room.

"Lee," he said, "we'll discuss those plans for the future when I get back."

"Have a good vacation, Uncle John. Don't worry about the office."

Liza's gaze moved from Mr. Wilson's back to the desk. Lee had already slipped into his uncle's chair and lifted a folder from the desk. *Make yourself at home,* she thought grimly. The phone rang, and as she reached for it, their hands collided. "I'm the secretary, remember? John Wilson, Attorney-at-Law. May I help you?"

She propped the phone on her shoulder, setting the cup on the desk as she moved the files, hunting for the one she needed. "No, sir. Not yet."

The stream of crude words being shouted into her ear made Liza wish she had the nerve to hang up on the man. "I know you want it now. The papers just arrived in this morning's mail. I can . . ." She frowned. "Okay, if that's what you want. If you can't wait, you'll have to see Mr. Hayden. Mr. Wilson's out of the office. Fine. I'll call you back with a date and time. Yes, I'll make sure it's this week."

The receiver bounced when she replaced it in the cradle. First, Mr. Wilson didn't even think he owed it to her to share his plans, and now the clients wanted someone else when she could help. She looked up, meeting Lee's gaze.

"You want to tell me what's wrong?"

"Nothing."

"Your face is too expressive."

She didn't like that he could read her so easily. "Don't mind me. Nobody tells me anything, but I'm expected to know everything," she announced in a fit of pique.

"You're upset about me," Lee guessed.

The fight left Liza, her voice growing soft as she said, "I'm sorry. I shouldn't take my frustrations out on you."

His look grew even more serious. "You don't have to apologize. I'm sorry, too. Uncle John shouldn't have sprung this on you. He values you highly. In fact, he feels you have a lot of potential going to waste in this one-lawyer office."

Her boss had voiced his sentiments on the matter numerous times. "Some people do better behind the scenes than in the spotlight. I like being a paralegal just fine."

"Don't sell yourself short," Lee warned. "Uncle John knows the law and how capable you are."

"Thanks, but I'll stay where I am."

"I'm glad to have you here. Did you get Barney and Fluff home unscathed?"

What a way to be remembered. "Dr. Wilson loaned me a cardboard carrier for Fluff. That's the last time I take those two anywhere together."

"I imagine Uncle Dennis took it all in stride."

Everything clicked into place. Dr. Dennis Wilson, the town's vet and Mr. Wilson's brother, was Lee's other uncle. There was a sister who had left town years before. She must be his mom.

"Thanks again for coming to my rescue."

"Rescuing a lovely lady is always a pleasure." He indicated the desktop. "Are you ready to tackle this? You mentioned appointments?"

Liza pulled a chair up to the desk. She'd thought about Lee Hayden several times over the weekend, but not even in her wildest imagination had she thought they'd be working together.

And work they did. Never before had Liza labored so long and hard. Used to Mr. Wilson's more laid-back "we'll get it done tomorrow" attitude, she found herself struggling to keep up with Lee's driving demands. He examined every client file with great care and capably handled a number of situations that arose.

Although Liza felt certain Lee asked no more of her than he felt she was capable of performing, she found herself stretching to reach heights never before attained. She even changed her working style to match his and stayed late to complete the work he assigned, all the time thinking his momentum couldn't last.

The Friday signaling the end of the first week proved to be one of those irritating days when no matter how hard she tried, Liza accomplished nothing. She typed until her arms and shoulders ached, all the while dealing with constant interruptions. The telephone seemed to ring every minute and unscheduled clients dropped by, hoping to take care of business while in town.

When she finished the page, Liza took a break, working out the kinks in her neck as she ran the spell-checker. Involved with the legal jargon, she didn't hear Lee enter her office.

"Did you finish the Johnson brief yet?"

"Can't it wait?" Liza asked, dreading the thought of starting another lengthy document.

"You need to finish it before you go." At

her disappointed look, his brow lifted, and he asked, "Can't you keep up?"

Resentful that he would criticize her competence, Liza snapped to attention. "If I couldn't, I can assure you I wouldn't be here, Mr. Hayden."

Lee waved a hand over her jumbled desk. "Then I can assume you plan to finish this tonight?"

Take it easy, Liza cautioned, forcing herself to take a deep breath. The downward sweep of long lashes dropped shutters over her hazel eyes. "Of course. It'll be on your desk within the hour."

After he left, she wasted precious seconds slamming folders around in her hunt for the right one. She knew her job. She'd been in this office for ten years, and he might be in charge now, but he wouldn't be in that role forever. Once Mr. Wilson got back, things would return to normal.

Liza laid the completed work on his desk exactly within the allotted hour.

"Good job," Lee complimented, signing his name with a flourish.

"Is that all?" she asked coolly.

He leaned back in the executive chair. "You're upset again. Why?"

Like he doesn't know the answer to that question. Liza permitted herself the luxury of a withering stare, lifted the stack of files, and marched from the room.

The file cabinet trembled when she jerked the drawer open. Determined not to leave one paper out of place, Liza quickly inserted the folders into the proper slots.

Lee followed, propping his hip on the edge of her desk. "What did I do?"

"I don't much care for being pushed," she snapped.

"I wasn't pushing."

"Right," came her sarcastic reply. She whirled about to face him. "I don't like having my ability questioned either. I don't work eighty-hour weeks. This is a small country town. We don't have hundreds of thousands of people, and those we do have aren't in as much of an all-fired hurry as you seem to think. Besides that, the Johnson trial isn't on the docket until next month. Monday wouldn't have made one bit of difference."

"I need to familiarize myself with the case."

In the course of her work, she had met a number of men but never one who exuded so much self-confidence. At times she was intimidated by his confident behavior, but not now. "Mr. Wilson will be back long before then. He knows the case inside out."

"I need to know it the same way."

His needs were beginning to get on her nerves. "Well, I need to go home and catch up on the chores I haven't been able to do this week."

"But I thought we would . . ."

Pushed to breaking point, Liza said, "I've done two people's work all week. I won't do it again. If that's the way you work, find yourself a new secretary."

She grabbed her purse from the drawer and started toward the door. Tears stung her eyes, blinding her.

"Liza, wait."

As Liza fumbled with the doorknob, Lee moved closer. He lifted her chin to look into her eyes and rubbed away the tears with his thumb. The wild flutter of her pulse when he smiled didn't surprise her.

"I'm sorry. Forgive me?"

"Sure." She felt embarrassed by her outburst. She would have never reacted to Mr. Wilson's requests in such a manner.

"Why are you conscience-stricken whenever you take a stand?"

"Because I feel guilty for treating you badly. My behavior just now was totally uncalled for."

"Your friends aren't going to stop liking you because you stand up for yourself. They aren't friends if they do."

Powerful relief filled her. "And are you a friend?"

"I'd like to be. Have dinner with me tonight."

It was more of a command than a request. When she hesitated, he prompted, "Say yes. This cruel boss wants to make amends to his hardworking assistant, and this man wants to see the beautiful woman he rescued last week."

The invitation was so tempting. "I can't," she admitted reluctantly. "I really do have chores waiting at home."

Lee frowned. "Don't you have hired help?"

"I wish. Right now, Daddy's in the field from dawn to dusk, and I'm helping by feeding the livestock. Mom usually does that chore, but she hasn't been feeling well this week."

"And thanks to me, the animals have been getting their evening feed quite a bit later than usual. When do you finish?"

"It takes about an hour."

"A late dinner sounds fine. Meet me at the restaurant next to my hotel at nine o'clock."

Liza examined Lee's face closely. Was he sincere, or was it a ploy to keep her sweet so he could work her even harder next week? Her men-judging skills were rusty, to say the least. Should she go? Why not take a chance? She nodded. "Okay."

He was obviously pleased. "See you then."

After leaving the office parking lot, her red sports car flew along the country roads. Anticipation had replaced her exhaustion, and she arrived in record time, somehow without managing to break the speed limit.

"Mom," she called when she entered the house.

Sarah Stephens came to stand in the archway to the living room.

"I'm going into town after I feed up and change. I'll eat there. Oh," she cried, stopping on the bottom stair, "what about you and Daddy? You aren't up to fixing supper."

"Go on. We're going to your grandmother's in a few minutes. I feel much better. Just a spring cold."

"Are you sure?"

"We'll be fine."

Liza changed into jeans before rushing out to feed the animals. "There, Barney," she said, pouring food into his bowl. The dog barked, blocking her way when she tried to move back to the barn. She brushed him aside. "I don't have time to play now."

Every chore seemed to take twice as long

as usual. After feeding the livestock, Liza raced back inside to shower and change. Glancing at the clock, she reached for the blow-dryer. She should have known better than to wash her hair. It took forever to dry.

Liza decided on a dressy pantsuit. After slipping her feet into sandals, she picked up a pair of earrings and tried to get them into her lobes while running down the stairs.

Doing a slow pirouette for her parents' inspection, she asked, "How do I look?"

"You look beautiful, honey," her father said, barely giving her a glance over his newspaper.

"Daddy," she groaned, leaning to kiss his weathered cheek. "I could be dressed in a clown suit, for all you know."

He dropped the paper and teased, "Seen you in one of those, too. You were pretty cute."

Liza grinned.

"Besides, I think you're beautiful no matter what you wear."

"Partial, I guess," she said, giving her mother a wink as she returned his hug.

"Tell Granny hello, and don't you overdo," she warned her mother. "See you later."

Lee found himself wondering if Liza was going to show up. He checked his watch and found it was still a few minutes before she was due.

Her reaction to his badgering had been a revelation. Miss Stephens might appear meek and mild, but when she got upset, she had quite a temper. He'd felt well and truly put in his place when she finished with him earlier.

Lee knew she was right. He had pushed her too far. He doubted Uncle John kept hours much beyond eight in the morning to five or six in the afternoon. She'd dealt with her normal workload as well as his requests for client files and research requests.

He hoped she'd understand that he was looking at the possibility of being in charge of his own destiny. The idea of being his own boss appealed immensely. Of course, his success depended on several factors.

Most importantly, he had to prove himself capable to his uncle. Family ties were strong, but Uncle John wasn't about to turn his clients over to an incompetent. Protecting his reputation was vital enough to make that his number one priority.

The hostess escorted Liza through the dimly lit room to his table. Lee admired Liza's understated elegance. Tonight she wore slacks and a blouse with appropriate jewelry

— all very modest, but something was different.

Her hair, he realized. Since he'd first been attracted to girls, long hair drew his attention. Tonight Liza wore hers in a fantastic rippling cascade of dark curls.

He smiled his greeting and stood to pull out her chair, fighting back the urge to touch her hair. "You look great. You should wear your hair down like this more often. It's beautiful."

"Thank you."

"Did you get everything finished at home?"

"Yes," she said, shaking out the mauve napkin.

"How's your mother?"

He could tell she was nervous by the way she sipped ice water and then glanced around, paying a great deal of attention to the decor.

"Better. She says it's a summer cold."

"Hope you don't catch one. Summer colds are really difficult to get rid of. Liza," he said softly, "what's wrong?"

She glanced down at the table. "It's me. I don't know what to expect."

"Why do you have to expect anything?"

"I just do."

Reaching for her hand, he squeezed gently.

34

"All right. What do you say to an amicable working relationship and an enjoyable evening?"

"I'd like that. I'm just not sure. . . ."

"Don't analyze everything to death. Tonight we're friends. Coworkers from nine to five. Or eight to whenever," he joked. "I'm really sorry about this week. Blame it on my personality."

Lee worked hard at making her feel comfortable. They sipped ice water and studied their menus, discussing the various entrées. They had just placed their order when a couple stopped by to say hello to Liza.

She introduced them as her best friends, Kitty Berenson and Dave Evans. "Lee's working at the office," she told them, adding, "He's my rescuer from last Saturday."

When her friend smiled and nodded, he knew the women had discussed him at some point.

"Kit, our table's ready," Dave said, slipping his arm about her waist.

"You're dining late," Liza said.

"Dave couldn't get away. He's promised to take me riding tomorrow to make it up to me. Say, why don't you join us? I'm sure Majesty could use the exercise. You should come, too, Mr. Hayden."

35

"The name's Lee, and I don't have a horse."

"I'm sure my brother would love it if you rode his. Sir doesn't get much exercise now that Jason's working all of the time."

"Name the time and place."

They made the arrangements, and after the other couple went to their table, Lee said, "So I get to see this horse that eats less than your dog?"

Liza laughed. "He's a pretty big fellow, too."

"And how does he feel about Fluff?"

"They tolerate each other."

"But you can't carry him underneath your arm." Reminded of Saturday's escapade, they laughed together.

"I'll be sure to tuck in my shirttail this time."

"I haven't ridden in a long time. Hopefully I won't make a fool of myself."

"You'd have to go a long way to look more idiotic than I did," she pointed out. "Besides, this will give you a chance to see some of the countryside. It's particularly beautiful this time of year."

"So tell me about being a farmer's daughter," Lee invited, pushing the appetizer tray in her direction.

Liza indicated she didn't care for any.

"How 'bout I show you tomorrow?"

"Think this city slicker is up to the experience?" Lee gave her a wide grin.

"It might give you an entirely different outlook on life."

He shrugged. "I'm pretty open to new experiences, but after this week, is it safe to put myself in your hands?"

"Nothing safer."

"Then it's a deal." Lee offered his hand over the table.

When Liza slipped her hand into his, Lee felt a tingle of anticipation at the thought of spending a day away from work with her.

CHAPTER 3

After stuffing clothes into the washer, Liza reached into the cabinet for the detergent bottle.

"Can you run me into town?" her mother called from the kitchen.

The cup overflowed, and the liquid ran over Liza's hand. "Mom, I don't have time. Can't it wait?"

"Not if you want Sunday dinner."

"Did you ask Daddy?"

"Forget it."

Liza heard her mother mumbling as she went into the pantry to dig around in the freezer. Her car would be in the shop today, of all days. If only Mom would drive hers, but the woman refused to drive the sports car. Liza pushed back the twinge of guilt and shrugged. Daddy would take her. He had said something at breakfast about picking up a tractor part.

Still, Liza couldn't help feeling guilty.

She'd never finish if she took time to go into town. Her bedroom was in shambles, and the outside chores needed to be done. Maybe her laundry and ironing could wait until one night next week. Why hadn't Kitty suggested riding earlier in the week? Better yet, why hadn't she suggested a Sunday afternoon ride?

A couple of hours later, Liza stood under the shower spray, trying to restore enough energy to get her through the afternoon. Everything was done, including the grocery shopping.

In the bedroom, Liza looked at the clothes that lay on her bed. Jeans and a plaid cotton shirt might not be high fashion, but they were comfortable and appropriate. She dressed and dug a pair of worn boots from the closet.

Braiding her hair, Liza recalled Lee's compliment and thought only briefly about leaving it down. Streaming in the wind, it was a nuisance when it whipped across her face and eyes.

Liza walked into the barn to get a bridle and came back to lean against the gate. She watched Majesty run in the paddock, his movements as fascinating as they had been the first time she saw him. The idea of having a show horse had intrigued her, but life got in the way of that venture; instead, she'd found he was a good horse for riding. She loved his graceful, perfectly coordinated steps.

Liza whistled, smiling when he came immediately. "You know we're going riding, don't you, boy?" she asked, rubbing his neck. Majesty nuzzled her shirt pocket in return. "Rascal." She fed him the horse candy, slipped the bridle in place, then led him through the gate and into the barn so she could finish saddling him.

The powerful roar of Lee's car engine could be heard coming up the road. Liza forced herself to linger in the barn. It wouldn't do for him to see how eager she was.

When the car door slammed and he called her name, she walked to the door and gestured him inside.

Lee hesitated when Barney raced toward him. "Are you sure he doesn't bite?"

"Only salesmen and city lawyers," she teased.

"Call him off."

Liza laughed. "Come on, Lee. He's gentle as a kitten."

"Yeah, Fluff would attest to that."

"Come here, Barney." Liza wasn't surprised when the dog failed to follow her command. She crossed the yard and buried her fingers in his thick coat to grab his collar.

Lee moved to her other side, giving the dog plenty of distance. He never seemed to be in a rush, even when he was in a hurry, yet she knew he was a dynamo rolled up into one neat package. For a second, she envied him his self-confidence, then she sighed. She couldn't have everything.

"Where's this fantastic horse?"

She indicated the hitching post by the barn. "Over here."

Lee followed, whistling low. "Beautiful animal."

"I knew Majesty was the one for me the minute I saw him," Liza admitted, petting the nose he thrust over her shoulder.

"Looks like he feels the same way," Lee said.

"He knows the good life, don't you, boy?" The horse whinnied in return. "Ready?"

Lee nodded, coming over to stroke Majesty's silky mane. He spoke softly to the animal before lifting his foot to the stirrup and swinging into the saddle. Gripping the reins securely, he held the horse still for Liza to mount.

"Not back there. Come up front so we can talk," Lee insisted.

41

"You'll be uncomfortable," she argued.

"Get up here."

"Okay," she murmured, "just remember whose idea it was."

"What's that?" he asked, indicating the plastic bag she held.

Liza pulled it to her. "A surprise."

"You'll spook the horse with that rattling."

"Majesty's not easily spooked."

He looked doubtful. "At least tell me what's in there."

"You'll see."

The bag held a kite, the old-fashioned kind, brilliantly colored in reds and yellow. She made the impulse purchase earlier in the week after she'd seen a child flying one. She wasn't even sure she'd ever get it off the ground. At least there was a breeze today.

Once on the horse, Liza sat stiffly, her muscles screaming for release. When she could fight it no longer, she let go and leaned her shoulders against Lee's chest.

"That's not so bad, is it?" he asked, his breath warming her ear.

"No," she agreed shyly.

As they rode along the meandering dirt track, Liza pointed out landmarks: an old house that had once housed tenant farmers, and the huge spreading oak she and Kitty had climbed as children. Lee asked about properties, and Liza indicated where one tract ended and the next began with the wooded area on the Berensons' place. "That's Kitty's house over there."

In the yard, he jumped down and reached for Liza, his hands firmly gripping her waist to swing her to the ground.

"Liz. Lee," Kitty called, hurrying across the yard. "Glad you could make it. Dave's saddling Sir now."

"Thanks for making it possible. Excuse me, ladies. I'll see if he needs help."

Both women watched his trek to the barn.

"Looked like you were enjoying yourself," Kitty commented.

"I was."

"Want me to tell him Sir's out of commission?"

Liza laughed, taking Kitty's arm and pulling her along. "You have the craziest ideas."

Dave and Lee were chatting like old friends when they led the horse from the barn. Dave greeted Liza, but she doubted he heard a word she said when Kitty struck up a conversation with Lee.

David Evans was a neighbor, another member of their terrible foursome. Of course, now that everyone was older and worked harder than they played, the good times were more memory than anything else.

The Evanses were farmers also, although on a grander scale than the rest of the neighborhood. They were considered pretty well-to-do, but their financial status had never made any difference in their friendship.

The fourth member of their group, Kitty's brother Jason, was married with a family of his own. Liza knew it was only a matter of time before Kitty and Dave married. They had been sweet on each other for as long as Liza could remember. Sooner or later, he would ask Kitty. Knowing Dave, he was trying to come up with the grandest proposal possible.

After mounting, the other couple rode on ahead, leaving Liza to follow with Lee.

"Where did you learn to ride?" she asked, reining Majesty in to ride alongside Sir.

"My grandparents kept a horse for me. Thought every self-respecting —"

Both were surprised when the horse started. Lee pulled up the reins, and Sir reared, unseating him.

Liza jumped down and ran to where he lay on the thick green grass. "Lee?" She grew frightened when he didn't respond immediately.

He groaned and said, "I warned you about that bag."

Relieved, she breathed deeply. "Kitty took the bag. There was a rabbit. I thought you saw it. Are you hurt?"

"Nothing seems to be broken." He moved his arms and his legs cautiously. "The fall knocked the breath out of me."

"Here, rest your head in my lap." She dropped to the ground. "Are you sure you're okay?" she asked again, concerned that he might be hurt worse than he realized. Liza stroked his hair in a comforting manner.

"I think so," he murmured, his tone growing strangely anxious. "Liza, I'm seeing double."

"What are we going to do?" she cried, looking about for help.

Moving closer, she missed the mischievous glint in his blue eyes. Liza jerked back when he kissed her. Her movement dislodged Lee, and he hit the ground with the unexpected movement. "Don't ever do that again, Lee Hayden," she ordered sternly, anger replacing her fright. "If you do, I'll . . . I'll . . . ," she began, only to find herself at a loss for words.

Lee reached to massage his head before leaning back on propped elbows. "Sorry. I couldn't resist."

"You scared me."

Her anger abated beneath the warm glow of his smile. "I won't do it again."

"See that you don't." Standing, she reached down to help him up. Lee took hold of her hand, pulling her off balance once more. She was barely able to keep the laughter from her voice as she broke away and got to her feet. "Stop playing. The others are waiting."

"Let them wait. I'm sorry I frightened you. Forgive me?"

She wasn't experienced in the ways of men, but this was one of the most mystifying she'd ever met.

"Sure. You take Majesty," Liza directed, avoiding his gaze. "I'll take Sir. And be careful. You could really get hurt next time."

"I'll keep Sir, if it's all the same to you."

Liza knew he was determined not to be defeated by the horse. She climbed into the saddle and looked down at him. "Are you sure you're okay? We can go back."

Lee patted her knee. "I'm sure. Let's find the others."

He captured Sir and mounted, riding off in the direction the others had gone. Liza guided Majesty into a running walk, gliding past them. In the spirit of competition, Lee urged his horse on and soon caught up with her. Minutes later, the pond came into sight and they reined their horses, dismounted, and walked to where the other couple sat.

Their childhood haunt had changed little over the years. The earth had revitalized itself in the green foliage and lush green grass. A strategic rope dangled from the huge shade tree near the pollen-coated pond, a tire swing in the lower branches.

Liza dropped Majesty's reins to the ground. The well-trained animal remained where he stood. "You'd better tie Sir," she suggested when Lee attempted the same. "He's not likely to stand around long if you don't."

After checking for spiders and testing the rope, Liza maneuvered her legs through the tire and leaned back, her feet touching the ground briefly before she kicked them into the air. The increasing momentum raised her high into the sky, giving her the sense of freedom she recollected from childhood. "I'm glad this is still here."

"Compliments of Mom and Dad," Dave said. "They ordered me to get the place ready for the grandchildren this summer."

Liza nodded, twisting in circles as she said, "Mickey's kids are just the right age to enjoy this place." She let go. The rope unwound itself, and she climbed out, dizzy.

Kitty slipped out of her jeans and shirt to reveal a one-piece swimsuit. She stretched out on the blanket to work on her tan. "What took you so long?" she asked when Liza's shadow blocked the sun. "Dave and I thought maybe you decided to go elsewhere."

"Majesty's been rowdy today."

"You probably need to ride him more often."

Liza nodded, glancing at Lee.

"Thanks," he whispered. "You saved my pride."

"I should have told on you."

"But you wouldn't, would you, sweetheart?"

"I still can," she warned. "Where's my bag, Kit?"

The woman pointed to the bottom of the blanket.

She looked up at the clouds scudding across the Carolina blue sky. "Perfect day for kite flying. Sure you don't want to help?"

"No, thanks."

Liza found herself a sunny spot and sat down. She laid the kite on the ground, then took out the string and tail.

Lee followed and sat down across from her. "This is the big secret?"

She nodded, stripped off the cellophane wrap, and unrolled the kite. Laying the sticks aside, she read the instructions, finding they made little sense to her mechanically challenged mind.

A pity Jason wasn't here. He'd always been in charge of their kite construction.

"Well, that's that," she said, giving up. "I should have gotten one of those pre-assembled jobs."

"May I?"

Liza hugged her knees. "Help yourself."

The instructions remained where she'd tossed them. Lee never glanced at the paper as he put the kite together and tied the string and tail in record time. "Want to run with it?"

Liza jumped to her feet and ran with the wind, frowning when the kite drifted to the ground each time she let go. "One more time," she called, lifting it over her head. She let out a whoop of joy when the wind carried the kite into the sky, taking it higher and higher on the string Lee unwound.

Liza's gaze touched on the bright colors that danced in the sky. There was something about flying a kite. But she wasn't really flying it. "Lee, can I . . ."

The hole that caught her foot was unseen. She fell face first on the ground and lay stunned, fighting to get her breath back.

"Liza?"

"Watch that last step. It's a doozy," she said, laughing at his shocked expression.

He stuck out a hand and pulled her to her feet. "Can we get on with this kite flying, or do you plan to lie around on your face the rest of the day?"

Liza wrinkled her nose at him.

The wind played with the kite, taking it higher. It soared and dipped, sometimes precariously close to the ground before the wind caught and carried it back. Shielding their eyes from the sun, they watched its antics.

"Why a kite?"

Her mouth curved in an unconscious smile. "It struck me as a fun thing to do."

"I think I was ten the last time I did this."

"Why so long?" she asked.

"It didn't fit in with everything else. I was too busy having a good time, and when I started work, I was too busy trying to make an impression."

"On whom?"

He concentrated on unwinding more string. "Nobody important. I realized there's more to life than making a name for yourself any way you can."

"I don't understand."

"Let's just say I didn't like the man I was becoming."

"So you've left that life behind you?" She trailed after him.

Lee handed her the string, flexing his arms. "I'll never go back to the way it was before. That much I know. Look out," he called when the kite caught a downdraft and crashed.

"Too late," Liza said, rolling the string into a ball as she walked over to where the kite lay.

"Want to try to fly it again?"

She knelt and examined the broken stick, a skeptical smile touching her lips. "This one is ready for wherever it is injured kites go."

"A little tape works wonders."

"You happen to have a little tape on you?"

Lee lifted his hands and shook his head.

Liza picked up the kite and walked toward the pond. "I'll leave it under the tree. We wouldn't want to spook Sir again," she teased with a cheeky grin.

"Just you wait until I get some tape," he threatened. "I'll make you run with the kite. Think your face can take it?"

Liza chuckled. At this rate, there was no way she'd ever impress him with her gracefulness. "I'd better not chance it."

Settling by the pond, she absently tossed pebbles, watching the ripples they made. Lee soon joined in, and they vied to see who could skip rocks the farthest. Liza conceded defeat when he outdistanced her time and time again. The sun bore down on them full force, and Liza slipped off her shirt to reveal the tank top underneath.

In the distance, she could hear Kitty's high-pitched demands that Dave stop tickling her feet.

"Where's your suit?" Lee asked.

"Home. I thought we were riding today."

Dave scooped Kitty into his arms and walked toward the pond. "Dave Evans, don't you dare," Kitty ordered. "I'll never speak to you again."

He feinted the drop, laughing when he swung the screaming woman to her feet at his side. Livid, Kitty stomped back to the blanket.

Stifling a grin, Liza glanced at Lee. "Dave just made a major mistake. Kit's serious about her sunbathing."

"Too serious," Dave agreed, dropping down beside Liza on the grass. "When does your father finish planting?"

"Monday or Tuesday." Her thoughts went to her dad and how busy he was. "He's been in the fields all week."

52

"Except for Sundays, this is the first time I've left the farm during the day in weeks." He glanced at Kitty. "I need to be home working now, but she'd kill me if I told her."

Liza sympathized, thinking of the amount of work there was to do on a farm the size of the Evanses'. The slightest delay could cost them. It wasn't only today he couldn't spare time. They would be extremely busy over the months ahead, as would every farmer in the county, including her father.

"Speaking to me yet, Kit?" Dave called when she sat up and looked at them.

"No," she snapped, lying back on the blanket.

He stood and walked toward her, his tone cajoling, "Come on, Kit. You know you want to."

Liza watched for a few minutes as Dave attempted to tease Kitty back into good humor. She was making him pay, but Dave was a charmer. He'd have Kitty saying she was sorry, if she didn't watch her step.

"Sounds like Dave has a fight on his hands," Lee commented.

"Kitty loves Dave. She has to accept his responsibilities."

Lee plucked a long blade of grass, examining it before he spoke. "What is it about farming that makes them keep at it? Why continue to work so hard and fight such a losing battle? What do they get out of it?"

Liza slanted her head to one side and studied him closely. "Farming's not only a business. It's a way of life. Daddy is the eternal optimist. He's willing to take the risks involved. He has so much faith in God's ability to grow that little seed that he's willing to make it his livelihood. A finished crop gives him a sense of satisfaction equal to, say —" she broke off, searching for the right way to make him understand. "To what you feel when you win a case you've worked particularly hard on. No matter how tough the winter, there's always promise of new growth in the spring."

"How can you work all day and go home to chores?"

"Most days, I get everything done, including taking care of Majesty, who is my responsibility anyway. I like to spend time with Daddy. After all, I'm the son he never had. He's taught me to do lots around the farm, and I let him because he doesn't have anyone else to pass it on to. He already tells me the farm is mine when he's gone."

"That throws a lot of responsibility on your shoulders. What happens when you decide to marry? Do you choose a farmer, or what?"

Liza laughed aloud, lifted her braid, and tossed it over her shoulder. She whistled for Majesty and climbed into the saddle. "That one's simple, Lee. No matter what his profession, I marry the man I love."

She urged Majesty into a run as the unusual restlessness pushed her. It was as if the animal understood her needs. Woman and horse raced along the farm road, churning up a cloud of dust. When she realized how far they'd come, Liza turned around. Reins in hand, she walked over to the edge of the pond where the others were gathering their stuff. "Are we leaving?"

"We thought you'd already gone," Kitty said. "Why did you take off like that? What were you two talking about anyway? I heard you say something about the man you loved."

"We were just getting to know each other."

"Lee has business in town. Dave's going to help with the horses."

"I'll take care of them," Liza volunteered. "I'm sure you and Dave could use some time alone."

Kitty giggled and suggested, "Take Sir home first, and then you take Lee back to your house to get his car."

"I could probably handle that," Liza said.

Majesty tossed his head over her shoulder and nosed her shirt pocket. "No more treats for you today." She started to move, as surprised as the horse when in his determination Majesty gave one final nudge and landed her in the pond.

Liza splashed about wildly, gulping a mouthful of water before her sense of balance reasserted itself and she kicked out of her panic. "Ooh, you," she yelled, blinking away the water that streamed into her eyes. Majesty raced off toward home, heedless of her repeated whistles.

Grabbing hold of a nearby plant, she placed her feet against the embankment in an effort to gain leverage to pull herself out. The plant was a puny specimen at best, and when the roots pulled out of the muddy bank, she landed with yet another gigantic splash. "Help," she implored, holding out a hand to Lee.

He pulled her from the pond, her feet slipping and sliding along the muddy wall. She was thankful to have both feet on the ground again.

"You're green."

The pollen gathered on the water clung to her skin. The absurdity of her appearance struck Liza, and she began to laugh. The more she thought about what had happened, the harder she laughed; soon she doubled over at the waist.

"Liza, are you okay?"

She forced herself upright, her chest aching. "I'm fine. I can't believe all this stuff is happening to me."

"How will you get home?" Dave asked.

"Walk. If you see Majesty, bring him back. Although I'm sure he's well on his way to the stable at home. Based on the way he was running, he's probably standing by the door already. Guess he's not used to me in green."

"You can't walk that far," Kitty objected.

"You want me hanging onto you? I'm a slime monster." At her friend's hesitation, Liza said, "I wouldn't inflict myself on any of you."

Lee spoke up. "Your shirt's over there on the grass, and you can wrap Kitty's blanket about your legs." A grin developed at their surprised looks. "Ever ride sidesaddle?"

"There's a first for everything, I suppose." Dropping to the ground, she pulled off her boots and dumped out the water. She tied the strings together and passed them to Lee. Liza pulled on the shirt and wrapped the blanket about her hips, complaining, "I feel like a mummy."

"At least you get to ride back with Lee,"

Kitty offered in a soft aside. "I couldn't have arranged it better myself."

Liza shook her head at her friend's logic. She tried to figure out how she was supposed to get from the ground to the horse. The blanket became a definite liability as she tried to hold on to it and lift one foot into the stirrup. She overbalanced, falling back onto the soft cushion of grass.

"I don't play fairy princess as much as I used to."

Lee's grin deepened into laughter. "Dave, we could use a hand."

Dave lifted her into Lee's arms.

"I'll bring Sir back later," Liza promised.

"No problem," Kitty said. "Glad you could make it, Lee. Liza, take care. See you at church in the morning." She paused and asked, "Have you found a church home yet, Lee?"

He shook his head, not expanding on the subject.

"We'd love to have you attend ours, wouldn't we, Liza?"

"I'll think about it. I've been too busy for church."

Too busy? His excuse raised a warning flag for Liza. She had heard many similar excuses over the years.

They waved good-bye and rode off across

the field.

Moisture from her clothes soon saturated the blanket. "I'm so sorry about this. I know you weren't expecting to ride home with a half-drowned female."

He shrugged. "Things happen. It's not your fault."

Minutes later, Lee stopped Sir in her yard. He flashed Barney a warning frown when he came running, his bark as spectacular as his bulk. "That animal is going to have us on the ground."

"Barney, hush," she ordered when the horse moved restlessly. "I said, be quiet," she repeated sternly.

"I don't trust him," Lee said when the dog ceased barking and sat down, his large brown eyes fixed on them.

Lee glanced at Barney once more before dismounting.

"Why?" she asked, slipping into his waiting arms. "He's just a big baby."

"Who's capable of taking a pretty big hunk out of anyone with whom he takes exception."

Dropping the blanket, Liza patted Barney's head. "Well, you'll have to see that you don't get on his bad side. I'm going to change clothes. Tie Sir over there."

Liza shed her jeans and caught sight of

herself in the bathroom mirror. She grimaced and lifted her sodden braid. Using a washcloth and soap, she wiped as much of the pollen from her face and arms as possible and grabbed a towel. In her bedroom, she wiped the towel over her hair and hurriedly dressed in dry clothes, aware Lee and the horses waited outside.

As expected, Majesty waited at the barn door. He whinnied at the sight of her, and Liza rubbed a hand along his neck. "I guess it wasn't your fault," she allowed, removing the saddle.

"How long is this going to take?" Lee took it from her hands and moved toward the barn.

She followed with the horses. "I'll do it. You have to get back to town."

"I can't leave you with all the work," Lee objected.

"I'm used to work. You can help next time."

"I really hate doing this."

"I understand," Liza said with a forgiving smile. "I'm glad you could come with us."

"I enjoyed myself."

"Everything?" she teased.

"Everything. See you at work on Monday."

She followed him to the barn door and waved good-bye as he opened his car.

Work, Liza thought, snapping her fingers. "Lee, wait. I forgot to tell you . . . ," she said, breathless after her run across the yard. "I have to be off Monday and Tuesday. Daddy needs me here."

"You can't."

"I have to," she insisted.

"We have a full calendar next week. The week after . . ."

"Won't work," she said before walking away. Did he think the crops could be put on hold until the office allowed her to be off? "Mr. Wilson approved my request before he left," she called back to him. "There's a temp coming in. If you can't survive, get a replacement. Fire me if you want. I don't care."

"Liza." He laid his hand on her shoulder. "I understand you feel you have to —"

"No, you don't," she interrupted. "If you did, we wouldn't be having this argument."

Barney growled, coming to his feet when Lee's expression grew angry. "If you'd just let me finish a sentence."

"Who's stopping you?"

"Be quiet," Lee snapped at Barney when he growled menacingly. His hand swept through his hair, exasperation lighting his eyes. "I can see I'm wasting my time talking to you. If you don't have any more concern

61

for the office than that, take two days, three, a week, the rest of the summer."

"I'll be glad when Mr. Wilson gets back," she called after him.

His car churned up clouds of dust as he raced down the driveway. He didn't understand. Maybe he couldn't. She didn't know. All she knew was, there was work to be done and she had to help.

By the time he reached the main road, Lee was convinced he had to be the biggest idiot in the state of North Carolina. What was he thinking?

Sure, he needed her help to keep the office going, but Liza was entitled to her approved vacation days. He'd always looked forward to R & R days. Though he couldn't see rest or relaxation in Liza's plan. Helping her father around the farm had to be exhausting.

What if she didn't return for the remainder of the summer? He wouldn't stand a chance. She had no idea how crucial she was to his success in the venture. In Charlotte, he was a little fish in a big pond, but here he hoped to be the prize catch.

From the first days Lee had worked with Liza, he knew they were a good team. Her knowledge level was invaluable. To her, the clients were her friends and acquaintances. As one of them, Liza understood their likes and dislikes, the diverse needs of farmers and business people alike.

For him to throw loyalty in her face was ridiculous. What had he done to deserve her allegiance?

In their one week as coworkers, her advice had kept him from antagonizing people . . . at least everyone but her. His foot rested on the brake momentarily. Should he go back and apologize? Somehow he doubted she was ready to hear it. Besides, he really did have to get back into town.

Lee depressed the accelerator and drove on. He'd ruined a wonderful afternoon with his behavior. He'd give her time to calm down, then he'd call later.

CHAPTER 4

Liza turned the page on her desk calendar and was jolted by the realization that Mr. Wilson had been away for almost four weeks. She could hardly believe it when Mr. Wilson called and lengthened his vacation by another two weeks.

The time had been spent getting to know Lee and experiencing his pleasure and displeasure at her responses to his demands. Her suspicion he wasn't a churchgoer had been confirmed when she mentioned her church again, only to have him tell her he didn't have time for that kind of thing. It certainly shed a new light on his behavior.

She struggled with the understanding and her growing attraction to Lee Hayden. The situation required plenty of knee time.

Beyond his call to apologize, Lee had not mentioned their argument again, but Liza had a gut feeling he felt she'd let him down.

At the time, she'd worried that Lee's reaction would be the same each time she requested a day off, but her dad hadn't needed her help again. She attributed that to the mention of Lee's negative reaction to her request. No doubt, he didn't want to cause her any problems at work.

Mr. Wilson was definitely coming back on Monday. He understood life in a small farming community. Lee had no idea what these people faced. Liza wondered why she even worried about how he felt and realized she wanted him to fit in. After that first week, she'd hoped they were becoming friends, but their differences would always serve as a wedge to separate them.

Liza finished straightening her desk, her thoughts on her plans for the weekend. She called good night to Lee and locked the door behind herself.

Her parents were visiting relatives while work on the farm permitted, and Kitty had invited herself over for the weekend. Liza almost laughed at the thought of Kitty promising to help with the chores if Liza went to the Evanses' cookout with her. She planned to go anyway, but Kitty's help was sure to make the work more interesting.

She glanced at the courthouse, appreciating its impressive dignity and historic significance. It sat on its island in the center of the traffic circle, with entrances to the building from all four directions.

Waving to some of the other people who worked in the area as they drove off, Liza hit the LOCK button on her remote and reached for the door handle. When the door didn't open, she glanced down and let out a horrified scream. Who could have done something like this?

She looked around to find herself alone in the parking lot. Running back to the office, Liza yelled Lee's name as she opened the door.

He charged from his office. "What's wrong?" When she didn't say anything, he grabbed her shoulders and demanded, "Liza, what's wrong?"

"My car," she whimpered, tears stinging her eyes. "Someone bashed in the driver's side. The door's jammed."

"Did they leave a note?"

"I don't know."

Lee pulled her over to the sofa. "Sit down. I'll check."

Liza couldn't sit still and trailed after him. Lee stooped beside the car, examining the damage.

"No note," he said when she bent down beside him.

"What do I do?"

"Wait until the police get here and have the car towed." He pointed to the worst damage. "You can't drive it with the fender on the tire like that."

Standing, she slammed a hand against the car hood. "Why? How could someone do this?"

Lee placed an arm about her shoulder. "Come on, Liza. I'll take you home after you give your report to the police."

Back in the office, she waited while Lee phoned the station. "They're dispatching a squad car. We need to wait outside."

The anticipation of the weekend was lost in the wave of emotion that overwhelmed her. A fresh wave of tears choked her every time she looked at the damage to her new car. Would it ever be the same again? No one could do that much damage and claim not to know.

It took a few minutes for the patrol car to arrive. "When did you find it, Liza?"

"Around five. After work. It wasn't like this at lunch. Do you think you'll find out who did it?"

"Hard to say." The officer concentrated on a streak of dark blue paint along the door. "We'll ask around to see if anyone witnessed the act. More than likely, not."

Liza's teeth clenched, feeling even more

furious that the offender would probably get off. "Why?"

"People who park here in the circle recognize your vehicle. If they'd seen the incident, they would have called you or the police."

"It makes me sick."

"Calm down, Liza," Lee urged. "It's just a car."

She eyed him. "My new car, Lee."

He hugged her close. "I know, but there's no sense in worrying now. The damage is done."

"It'll never be the same again."

"The body shop will make it as good as new. Let me take you home."

"We'll let you know if we hear anything," the officer said after checking to make sure the report was complete. "Where do you want it towed?"

Liza named the dealership where she had recently purchased the vehicle. Lee took hold of her arm and guided her to his car.

"Wait here. I'll lock up the office."

As they rode along, she had the strongest feeling of a child deprived of her favorite toy. She didn't want to pout but couldn't help herself.

For years, she'd driven her mother's old car. A breakdown had placed her in the dealership waiting area. The flashy red sports car spoke to her the moment she laid eyes on it. Though it was too expensive and more car than she'd needed, Liza had signed over a portion of her savings and received a fat payment book in return for the joy of driving her dream car.

The car had been another of her life changes. Everyone speculated on what had gotten into her, trading a paid-for compact that was good on gas for a fancy sports car. Now it was just another wrecked car.

"Liza? We're here." Lee parked in the yard.

She managed a weak smile. "Thanks for your help."

"Looks like Kitty's waiting."

"She's spending the weekend." Liza climbed out of the car.

"I'm glad you won't be alone."

She frowned. "I'm ticked off, not suicidal."

"I didn't mean it like that. Are you going to the Evanses' barbecue?"

"I don't feel like it."

"You need to get your mind off the car. With any luck, they'll find whoever did it."

Hope leaped in her. "You think so?"

He quickly averted his gaze, and she knew Lee was only trying to make her feel better. "Maybe. I don't know. But it's already happened. Don't let it spoil your weekend. See you at the Evanses'?"

She could hardly lift her voice above a whisper to answer him. Why did she feel this way? Was she too attached to a material possession? Probably.

Kitty came over to speak to Lee.

"You're kidding!" she exclaimed when Liza explained why she was late. "A hit-and-run accident at the courthouse, and no one saw it? There were a million cars up there today. Surely someone saw something."

"Yeah," Liza agreed. "The person who dragged his car alongside mine saw plenty."

In the kitchen, she opened the refrigerator and dug around until she found a chocolate layer cake.

"Liza, you don't want that."

The knife slipped through the cake, and Liza lifted the wedge onto a plate. "Don't tell me what I want. I'll eat the whole thing if the mood strikes me."

Kitty propped her hands against her hips and said, "Don't take this out on me, Liza Stephens. I didn't hit your precious car."

Liza shoved the plate away, dropping the fork with a clatter. Kitty was right. She didn't want the cake, and she shouldn't take her bad mood out on her friends. "I'm sorry. I'm just so angry."

"Of course you are." Kitty paused for a second. "Want me to call my dad and ask who he recommends for the bodywork?"

"I had them tow it to the dealership. Daddy will be back Sunday. I can ask him. I need to call Jason."

"He'll be at the cookout. You can tell him then."

Liza sighed. "Looks like I'll be thumbing for a few days."

"Kitty's taxi at your disposal — for the right price, of course."

Liza laughed. "The only thing I'm paying you is no attention. I seem to recall a certain crumpled fender that put you in Liza's taxi for a few days."

"That sounds like a pretty reasonable price," Kitty agreed.

Later, as they changed for the cookout, Liza considered her attitude. It was hard to smile, but she had to fight the depression.

"Lord, forgive me," she whispered. "I know I shouldn't feel this way about a car, but I can't help myself. Lift up my spirits and help me forgive the person who did this."

Going to the closet, she pulled out a white-and-lilac-striped sundress and slipped it on. She brushed her hair and left it hanging down her back.

The party was in full swing when they arrived, people milling around as they waited

71

for the hamburgers, steaks, and ribs to cook. The scents were mouthwatering.

Liza spotted Jason across the yard and waved.

Jason Berenson was Kitty's brother. Older than the two of them by barely a year, he was married and the father of an adorable six-month-old baby girl.

"Looking for someone in particular?" she teased when Kitty eyed the crowds.

"Not particularly."

"You don't fool me. I know Dave's around somewhere and the minute he lays eyes on you, you'll be his for the night."

Kitty waggled her left hand. "He hasn't put a ring on my finger yet."

"It's just a matter of time, and you know it."

"Well, time has a way of changing things."

Sure does, Liza thought as she followed Kitty over to where Jason stood. Kitty patted her brother's stomach, the extra pounds revealed by the sport shirt he wore. "Time to start working out, Jace."

"Good to see you, too, Kit."

"Well, brother, you're a young man, but if you want to let yourself go . . ."

"I start working out tomorrow, thank you," he growled.

"Glad to hear it. Guess we'd better track

down our host and hostess and say hello. By the way, Liza needs to report an automobile accident."

Kitty's words focused Jason's attention on Liza. His company insured all of the Stephenses' family vehicles. "Were you hurt?"

Liza shook her head. "Hit-and-run."

"That stinks. Don't worry. We'll make it good as new."

"Thanks, Jason. I'll be in touch Monday. Talk to you again later."

A mixture of successful business people and farmers filled the room. Some chatted in small groups while others danced to the music that blasted. Another group played basketball at a goal attached to the outside building. Others took advantage of the pool, and Liza wished she'd thought to bring her suit.

Dave came over and demanded, "What took you so long? I was beginning to think you'd decided not to come."

"Liza didn't get home till late," Kitty said. "Someone hit her car in the parking lot."

He looked at Liza for the first time. "Did you get his name and insurance company?"

"No such luck." She explained the situation as she looked around for Lee.

Dave let out a soft whistle. "Sorry, Liza.

You haven't had that car long, have you?"

"Four months."

"Let's change the subject," Kitty suggested.

"Come say hello to Mom and Dad," Dave said. Allowing him to lead the way across the yard, they chatted for a while before Dave and Kitty went off to dance. Liza left them to wander around the yard on her own. She caught sight of Lee among the group playing basketball and stopped to watch.

"Time out," Lee called when he spotted her on the sidelines. He grabbed a towel and wiped his face.

"Good game?"

He nodded and gave her a one-armed hug. "Feeling better?"

Liza felt her chest tighten in anticipation. Maybe he did understand after all. "I wanted to apologize for acting like a baby."

He smoothed a strand of her hair before allowing his fingers to glide down the length of her face. His gentle touch was almost an embrace. "You acted normal, given the circumstances."

"Come on, Lee," the other players called, but he lingered for a second longer, reassuring her once more that the car could be repaired.

"Lee, you're holding up the game," the others cried in protest.

"Later," he promised with a wink before jumping back into the action. Liza watched him snatch the ball and fly upward, pushing it into the basket.

Be thankful he stopped to speak, she told herself glumly. Sinking onto the end of a nearby bench, she watched Lee. What was it about him that made her want his attention?

A scream left her lips as Liza found herself on the ground, the other end of her bench becoming airborne.

"I'm sorry," her seat partner exclaimed. Liza allowed him to pull her to her feet and jumped away just in time to avoid being hit by the unattached plank. It tumbled to the ground at her feet.

Smoothing her dress over her hips, she sneaked a peek around, seeing the looks of concern and then amusement on everyone's faces. Heat filled her face. "Hope you enjoyed the entertainment," she muttered.

"Are you okay?" the guy asked.

For the first time, Liza took a better look at him. Something very familiar about his face tugged at her memory. His obvious concern made her feel better. She nodded and said, "Now that I have two feet under me."

"Dad's going to demand a reimbursement of my college tuition for engineering such flimsy seating."

Liza glanced at the cinder blocks that held the board. No doubt, when he stood, he broke the seesawlike balance, leaving her end to hit the ground.

Dad . . . That was what he'd said. Surely it couldn't be. Not after all these years. "Rick?"

Recognition brought a smile to his face. He gathered her in a hug. "I'd recognize that blush anywhere. Hello, Liza."

"I can't believe it," she said, throwing her arms about his neck. If possible, he was even more handsome, his boyish charm more refined. "It's been forever."

Her companion regarded her with amusement, his arms supporting her waist.

"Only fourteen years," he protested. "Are you happy to see your old flame?"

"Old flame?" Liza scoffed. "I wasn't even allowed boyfriends."

"Well, you had one, and it was me. How could I forget? You and Kitty followed me everywhere. Not even Dave and Jason could tempt you and Kitty away. You had this same long black curly hair," he said, tugging one of her curls, "and those beautiful braces on your teeth."

"At least the braces are gone," Liza said, flashing him the straight white teeth her parents had worked so hard to pay for. "Not to mention a few of those pounds you were polite enough not to mention."

He stepped back and took a look. "I like what I see."

"Oh, Rick," she faltered.

"I always loved that," he said. "You blushed at the least little thing."

"And you were always doing something to make me blush," she accused. "Who'd have ever thought you'd look like this?" she mused, laughing at his taken-aback expression.

"Thanks loads," he said, tweaking one of her long curls.

Rick had never cared much for having his picture taken, and it had been difficult to tell what he looked like since most of the photos she'd seen over the years involved a hard hat and a foreign locale. His mother declared the only time she got to see his face was when she traveled to wherever he was to visit him.

"Think nothing of it," Liza said, taking his hand and leading him through the crowd. "Come with me. I want to surprise Kit." Her laughter floated as he quizzed her on the past, dwelling on her devotion to him. "I'm sure I never did anything like that," she denied when he accused her of threatening to follow him to college. "Kit, look who's here. Why didn't you tell me Rick was home?"

Kit lifted her shoulders in defeat, shaking her head. "I didn't know. No one said a word."

"They didn't know I was coming," he said. "I surprised them all when I called to be picked up from the airport."

Kitty hugged him exuberantly. "How long has it been?"

"Liza and I agreed on fourteen years," he said, glancing at her for confirmation. "She fell all over herself welcoming me."

"He dumped me on the ground. Some men will do anything to pick up a woman."

His laughter sounded rich, warm, and deep. "Our Liza's grown up."

"We both have," Kitty said, slipping her arm about his. "Tell us what you've been doing all this time."

"Seeing the world. Using my engineering degree to take the jobs I wanted."

"So we heard," Liza said. "No thanks to you. Why didn't you write?"

"I was too busy," Rick said. "I remember how you two reacted to my news. You were shocked that I'd consider leaving the country life behind."

"And us," Kitty defended. "We didn't understand why you wanted to become an engineer when you had the farm here waiting for you."

"Dad was a pretty self-sufficient guy. Besides, my heart was never in farming. Not like Dave's. This way we both do what makes us happy."

"And now?"

His gaze stopped on Liza as the question popped out, his lazy smile warming her heart. "I'm between jobs and home for a long-overdue visit. All these guys had better watch out." He wrapped his arms about their shoulders and hugged them to him. "I'm going to stake my claim on my girls."

"I still can't believe it," Kitty said with a laugh. "Just wait until I see David Matthew Evans."

"Don't be too tough," Rick kidded. "He remembers how you acted when I was around. Probably thought you'd go tearing off to find me."

"I would not have," Kitty denied hastily.

Liza smiled, shaking her head. "No good, Kit. He remembers how we used to chase after him, called us perfect little fiends."

"Did he now?" Kitty demanded playfully.

"Never. I'd be happy to take you two anywhere."

"Who wouldn't?" a familiar voice questioned.

Rick turned to look at Lee. "I don't know. If they're still like I remember, it could be trouble with a capital T. Do you remember the night I said you girls couldn't come on my date? She was pretty angry when you popped up from behind the seat and told her I took you everywhere."

"Ladies, you didn't?"

"Well, she wasn't good enough for him," Kitty defended.

"I seem to recall she was homecoming queen and the bank president's daughter."

"We never could figure out why you preferred her to us," Kitty teased. Without so much as a blink of an eye, she flashed Rick her irresistible smile and rested her red-tipped fingers against the tanned muscles of his arm.

Watching her is an education, Liza thought. Kit flirted outrageously, spinning her web while she stood by, wondering at her friend's feminine wiles. *Just once, I wish I could attract men like Kitty does.*

"Rick shouldn't tell everything he knows," Kitty said in a silky voice. She winked at

Liza. "We could tell a few stories of our own."

"No, you couldn't." Rick placed a hand over her mouth.

"Old friends?" Lee inquired.

"I'm sorry," Liza said. "Rick Evans, Lee Hayden. Rick is Dave's older brother. Lee is Mr. Wilson's nephew."

"Nice to meet you." Lee reached out to shake hands.

"My pleasure," Rick said.

"I'm going to steal Liza away." Lee tugged on her arm. "There are a couple of burgers over there with our names on them."

Too startled by his suggestion to offer any objection, Liza went along. "Don't let him get away, Kitty," she called over her shoulder.

"I'm going to throttle Dave for not telling us Rick came home."

Her gaze followed them to the middle of the crowd. Kitty's hands wrapped about Dave's neck, and he was offering an earnest explanation while Kitty nodded doubtfully.

"How long have you known Rick?" Lee asked.

"A very long time. We grew up together."

"Together?" Lee repeated with raised brows. "He's what? Thirty-five? Thirty-six?"

"Only thirty-two," she corrected. "Kitty

and I adored him. He chauffeured us to the beach, took us riding — taught us to ride, for that matter. He did just about everything we wanted. Of course, we harassed him into a lot of it."

"That was mighty agreeable of him," Lee said.

"He's a mighty agreeable person. Kit and I cried for days when Rick went off to college."

"How long is he home for?"

His seemingly casual question struck her as odd. "I don't know. Why?"

"Perhaps I don't want him stealing my assistant away."

Leave it to Lee. His curiosity only extended to her capacity to do her job. "That's an idea. I always wanted to travel."

"Don't even think about it." Lee's gaze fixed on her face. "We need you far too much for you to go off gallivanting around the world."

Liza concentrated on picking up a Styrofoam plate, not wanting Lee to see how hurt she felt.

"Okay, what's wrong? What did I say this time?"

Liza hated being so transparent. "It bothers me when you decide the good of the office is more important than my happiness."

"I was joking." His defensive words struck home.

"Call it what you like," Liza said. "Everything's work to you. Your life revolves around the office."

Lee took her hand and pulled her over to a private corner of the yard. "I don't know what's going on in your head right now, but I don't care more about the office than you."

"You do." Raw nerves made her far too emotional to get into this with him now. Her wayward tongue refused to be silenced. "Every time I make a decision you feel doesn't work for the 'good' of the office, you retreat behind a wall. I'm glad Mr. Wilson is coming back on Monday."

"Well, Miss Liza, I've got a news flash for you: Uncle John might be coming back, but not long term. He's talking retirement and looking for someone to take over. I'm his man."

His words hit her hard. Didn't all the years she'd invested in the office entitle her to know what her boss was planning? Unable to speak, she turned and walked away. She didn't care if she ever saw Lee again. He had taken too much pleasure in dropping the bomb on her, and it hurt, terribly.

"Liza, wait!"

Even now, he sounded exasperated. What

did he expect? Did he think she would leap with joy at the prospect of having him as her employer? She blundered into Rick's arms. "Liza? What's wrong?"

"We seem to keep bumping into each other," she said with forced gaiety, her overly bright laughter bordering on hysteria.

"What happened?" he demanded, shaking her gently.

She saw Lee standing over by the shrubbery, watching them. In that moment, she knew her feelings for him were far stronger than she cared to admit. But it was senseless. She was part of the office machinery — a necessary evil.

"I shouldn't be here. Take me home, Rick. Please."

"What about Kitty?"

"She'll come later. She drove," she explained, sniffing as she knuckled away tears. "Rick," she exclaimed. "I'm sorry. It's your party. You can't leave. I'll catch a ride with someone else."

"No, wait for me in Dave's car. I'll get his keys and tell Kitty we're leaving."

"Thanks, Rick." She flashed him a tremulous smile.

"It's okay, baby," he comforted and offered a consoling hug.

Being there reminded Liza of the times

she'd been hurt as a child and he'd done the same, and somehow it made a difference. "You called me that when I was little," she reminisced.

"I did, didn't I?" he said, wiping tears from her cheek. "Old habits are hard to break. I'll meet you at the car."

He disappeared around the corner of the house, and she walked toward the car.

"Liza, don't run away," Lee said. "Let's talk this out."

Anger seemed to grow, mainly at herself for not having seen this coming. She should have recognized her need to impress him for what it was — attraction. The simultaneous excitement and fear she felt when she was near Lee was so obvious. How could she have been so stupid?

"Stay away from me, Lee Hayden," she cried, breaking into a run. "I never want to see you again. Do you hear me?"

Inside Dave's car, she rested her head in her hands and moaned, "I can't stand it."

Rick shut his door quietly, turning the key in the ignition. "Can't stand what?"

She sat up in the seat and declared, "The way people take advantage of me." Her eyes drifted shut for a minute. "That's rich. You should be angry with me." Liza sniffed. "I drag you away from your cookout and then have the colossal nerve to talk about people using me."

Rick concentrated his attention on getting past the vehicles parked in the yard. "You obviously needed to get away. Want to talk about it?"

Liza shook her head and huddled miserably in the passenger seat. Rick tried to start a conversation, then gave up when she failed to participate. Liza chastised herself for her behavior, but she couldn't respond — not until she figured out how to deal with the situation.

He turned onto the driveway leading to her house.

"I'm sorry, Rick. It's been an awful day. I never should have gone tonight."

She couldn't tell him she was falling in love with Lee. She couldn't tell anyone that out of all the men who were looking for a woman to love and cherish, she had to fall for the one who considered her no more than an office fixture.

"When you're ready to talk, I'll be here."

The corners of her mouth lifted in a grateful smile. Thank God he wasn't angry with her. She didn't think she could bear much more. "You always were a good friend."

Liza glanced toward the house and saw the uniformed patrolman pounding on their back door. "They found the person who hit my car!" She jumped from the car almost before it stopped completely. Maybe, just maybe, something in this horrible day was going to go right for her.

CHAPTER 5

"Liza, wait."

Ignoring his caution, she dashed across the yard to where the patrolman, a young officer she recognized from court, stood. "Did you find him, Bill?" she quizzed, her breath coming in deep, uneven gasps.

"Find who?" he asked.

When Rick joined them, she quickly became aware of the look the two men shared — the officer's almost apprehensive, Rick's curious.

"The man who hit my car," she wailed.

"I don't know anything about your car. They asked us to contact you. . . ."

A flicker of apprehension coursed through her at his expression. Fear drove her urgent demand. "Why are you here?" The volume of her voice increased to a near shout.

"Your parents were in a car accident. Your daddy had a heart attack."

She gasped, whispering a quick prayer that

they were okay. "Is he . . . ?" she asked brokenly, unable to finish the sentence. Vaguely aware of Rick's comforting arms about her, Liza asked almost incomprehensibly, "Mama?"

"She managed to get help. From what we can tell, Mr. Stephens was driving when it happened. They hit the ditch going pretty fast, and she was thrown out of the truck."

Bugs charged against the yellowing glare of the porch light. Crickets chirped in unison while Barney barked in the background and Majesty whinnied in his stall. *It can't be true,* Liza thought. Soon Rick would go home, she'd go to bed, and tomorrow would be a better day.

"Liza?" Rick shook her out of her withdrawn state.

"How badly were they hurt?"

The man's distaste for his duty was evident in the way he carried out the task. "I don't know. I'll take you to the hospital so you can talk to the doctor. He'll be able to tell you more."

"Which hospital?" Rick asked.

"The one here in town. They were almost home."

Goose bumps popped up on her arms. "Home?" She looked at Rick. "They weren't due back until Sunday."

"Whenever you're ready," the patrolman said.

More than a little tempted to grab her bag and go, Liza refused. "I appreciate the offer, but I'll need transportation later."

"Are you okay to drive? I know this was a shock for you."

"Go ahead," Rick told the patrolman. "I'll stay with her."

Still he hesitated, his eyes speaking his concern. "I'm sorry I had to be the one to bring you bad news, Liza. Call if you need anything?"

"Yes, of course," she assured, managing a smile. "And Bill, pray for them."

Rick took the house key from her shaking fingers and unlocked the door. He steered her toward the stairs. "Change and call Kitty. I'll do a quick check outside."

Feeling numb as the reaction began to set in, she agreed.

It was nice having Rick to rely on. After replacing her dress with jeans and a shirt, she dialed the Evanses' house and got their answering machine. No doubt they were all outside. She left a quick message, hoping someone would let Kit know. Liza turned the lights off and found Rick coming out of the barn.

"Ready?"

Liza could barely lift her voice above a whisper. "I couldn't reach Kitty. Maybe I should pack a bag? They'll need some things."

"The hospital will provide what they need for now. They're going to be okay," he reassured, dropping his arm about Liza's shoulders and pulling her close.

Trusting eyes met his as she whispered, "They just have to be."

He nodded, helping Liza into the car. His regard felt gentle and comforting, as did the hand that squeezed hers. Liza prayed throughout the long, nerve-racking journey.

"I'm Liza Stephens," she told the nurse at the emergency room desk. "My parents, Paul and Sarah Stephens, are here."

"Wait over there. I'll tell the doctor you've arrived."

Dr. Mayes came out shortly and gestured her over to a door just inside the waiting area.

"I came as soon as I heard. How are they?" She found his calm maddening as she waited for an answer.

"Settle down," he said with a reassuring pat on her shoulder. "Your father suffered a heart attack and fractured his leg. We'll know more about the severity of his heart attack in a few days."

"And Mama?"

"She was thrown from the truck on impact. Sarah managed to get help before blacking out. We're waiting for her to regain consciousness. She has some superficial face cuts and a couple of cracked ribs. We'll know more when she wakes."

"Can I see them?"

"Your father. For a few minutes. Reassure him about your mother if you can. Worrying won't help him."

Liza tried, but her father felt convinced his wife was worse than they were telling him. His agitated state did more harm than good, so the doctor finally ordered a sedative.

"Pray for her, Daddy," Liza whispered, squeezing his hand.

The nurse asked Liza to step out of the room.

Liza didn't know how to reassure him. Her own worry kept her from thinking clearly. Wearied by her indecision, Liza leaned against the wall in the hallway. She swiped away a tear just as the nurse exited the room.

She recognized Mrs. Timmons from church. The woman patted Liza's shoulder reassuringly and said, "He'll be fine. You can go back in."

Familiar brown eyes pierced the distance between them. "Honey, you'd tell me if anything was wrong, wouldn't you?"

The medication began to take effect, and he calmed down, almost falling asleep. "Yes, Daddy."

This was the first time she'd ever seen her father this low. She needed his strength, but right now it seemed she had to be strong enough for her parents.

The nurse returned to check on him and allowed Liza to remain by the bed until he dozed off.

In the waiting area, she found Rick and explained what she knew.

"I got a message to Kit. They wanted to come, but I told them not to. Dave promised to run over and check the farm tomorrow."

She nodded absently, pacing the small waiting area. Her head throbbed from the worry about her mother and the added stresses of the day. Would Mom recover? Being unconscious like this couldn't be a good thing.

"You've got to sit down. You're wearing yourself out."

Liza massaged her forehead in an attempt to rub away the agonizing pain. "That's exactly what I want," she confessed. "To be so tired I can't think about anything."

"You can't," Rick reasoned. "You have to remain clearheaded enough to make any decisions that have to be made. Come here." He reached for her.

Liza placed her hand in his, trusting him completely.

"Sit here and rest your head on my shoulder. Try to catch a few minutes' sleep. I'll wake you the minute I hear anything."

"I don't think I can."

"Try."

Even though she considered it impossible, Liza soon fell into an uneasy sleep, troubled by nightmares of her parents and Lee.

"Liza, wake up." Rick shook her lightly. Surprised, she lifted her drowsy gaze to his face.

"Your mom regained consciousness."

She looked to Dr. Mayes for reassurance. He nodded and smiled. "She's still in guarded condition. She has a slight concussion, but everything looks good."

"Thank You, God," Liza breathed. "Does Daddy know?"

"No. He's still asleep. They moved him to coronary care about two hours ago."

Two hours. Liza looked at the clock on the wall, not believing she had slept so long. "Can I see Mom?" She needed to reassure herself.

The doctor nodded. "She's been asking for you. I don't think she believes me when I say your dad is okay. My patients will hate me, but I might as well make rounds while I'm here."

Rick grinned, watching the old doctor disappear down the hallway. "He hasn't changed."

"Not a bit," Liza agreed. "Want to come with me?"

"I'll wait until she's better." Rick chuckled and explained, "Seeing me after so long might be an even greater shock."

"She'd be delighted. You always held a special place in her heart."

"Not today. Go ahead, and I'll take you home afterwards."

Through the window at the end of the hall, Liza could see the sun coming up. The activity in the emergency area had lessened little overnight. The constant stream of sickness and injury kept the staff busy and the waiting room chairs full.

"Thank You, Lord," she whispered again, taking a second longer to pin on a bright smile before pushing the cubicle's curtain aside. Liza fought to regain her fragile control at the sight of her mother's pain-filled eyes. "Mom," she whispered, her throat tightening. *Superficial?* Those cuts

95

looked terrible, and her face was black-and-blue.

"Liza," she called anxiously, "is your dad okay?"

"Daddy's fine. What were you two up to this time?" Liza asked, her voice growing stronger. She teased her parents often, saying they reminded her of a couple of teenagers with some of their antics. They were still so much in love.

"Paul wasn't feeling well, so we decided to come home early. It was terrible, honey," her mother said as she suppressed a shudder. "He grabbed his chest and slumped over the wheel. It happened so fast."

"It's okay," Liza comforted, resting her hand gently on her mother's shoulder for fear that she would hurt her further. Tears at the thought of almost losing them caught in her throat. "I've talked to Daddy. He's doing fine."

The woman tried to rise up on the bed, gasping with the pain that hit her. "Is he really? Please, tell me."

"They gave him a sedative, and he's resting," Liza answered easily. "He's worried about you, of course."

"How bad is he?"

There was no way to sugarcoat the harsh reality of what had happened. Her mother expected the truth. "He had a heart attack. The doctor doesn't know how severe yet. His leg's broken, too."

The woman's eyelids fluttered shut. "Mom, I'm going to leave so you can rest," Liza said softly. "Do you need something for pain?" At her mother's refusal, she said, "Get some rest. I'll be back later today."

"Are you okay?" she asked, warming Liza's heart with her motherly instinct. "I'm sure the news frightened you."

Liza dared not mention the emotional rollercoaster she'd been on before hearing the news. "Yes. God is in control. He's taking care of things. You concentrate on getting better."

Her mother's hold tightened. "Get Kitty to stay with you until we come home."

Liza leaned over to kiss her forehead. "I will. I've got a lot of people looking out for me. Oh, and guess who's home?"

"No idea," she countered weakly.

"Rick," Liza said. "He's with me now. I was at the Evanses' cookout, and he brought me home. Isn't that wonderful news?"

"I'm so happy for his family. His mother's been worried about him for some time. We pray for him every week."

"He looks really good."

"I'm sure you noticed," her mother commented, managing a feeble chuckle.

"Mother!"

There was an underlying teasing in her pain-filled gaze. "Tell him he must come see me."

"I will," Liza promised, kissing her cheek. "Love you," she called as she started out the door.

"I love you, too, baby," she responded tearfully. "Go home and get some rest. Your dad and I will be fine."

Her mother's words of welcome delighted Rick, and he ushered Liza home without giving her the opportunity to change her mind.

"Rest," he ordered, placing a light kiss on her cheek after he opened the front door.

She smiled gratefully. "I plan to. Thanks, Rick. I don't know what I'd have done without you."

"My pleasure."

No doubt he felt as exhausted as she did. "Be careful driving home."

As much as sleep appealed, Liza knew top priority was the number of telephone calls that had to be made.

"No, Granny, that was all he said," Liza told her mother's mother a second time. "They were both resting when I left the hospital. I'm going to do some things around here and go back later."

"Will you come stay with me?"

"I think it's better if I stay here. I'll get Kit to come over. Will you be all right?"

She listened as the woman went on for a few more minutes about her parents and her being alone in the house.

"I'm perfectly okay. I'll see you at the hospital later. Sure you don't want me to pick you up? Okay then, give Gramps my love."

Kitty said she would call later to see what time she wanted her to come over and made Liza promise to call the moment she needed anything.

"I'll have Mom call the pastor for you," Kitty added. "I'll be sure they activate the prayer chain."

"Thanks, Kit," she said, reaching up to push several strands of hair out of her face. "I'll talk to you later."

One more call. She dialed her boss's home number, deciding it might be the last opportunity she had over the weekend. He was very sympathetic and told her to take as long as she needed to get her parents situated. "Give them my regards."

"I will, sir."

"Liza, call if you need anything."

"Thanks, Mr. Wilson."

Relieved, she hung up the phone and fixed herself a sandwich and cup of cocoa. Upstairs, she slid into her nightgown and fell into bed, exhausted.

At first light the next morning, Lee drove up the road to Liza's house with no idea of what he hoped to find once he arrived. Maybe she had been there all night, ignoring the million or so messages he'd left.

Her reaction last evening before she drove off with Rick Evans frightened him. All night long Lee tried to reach her, only to have the phone ring the requisite number of times before her voice came on to recite the answering machine message.

And all because he'd opened his big mouth too soon. Or maybe too late. When he and Uncle John discussed the situation, they agreed to wait until Lee made a final decision. His uncle urged him to carefully consider whether he would be happy in a smaller town.

He knew full well Liza wasn't happy about her boss's choice to invite him into the firm in the first place. That fact led him to believe Uncle John's failure to bring her up to date on what they planned hurt her even more.

He felt very guilty for throwing the news

in her face like that. Her pained expression along with the words that she never wanted to see him again cut deep into Lee's heart. He needed her now more than ever, and he knew it had little to do with the office.

Seeing her with Rick last night scared him. She seemed so comfortable around her old friend, certainly more at ease than with him.

Lee parked, and Barney greeted him. He hesitated, not sure he wanted to test Liza's theory about the dog's gentleness, but the need to know forced him from the car. He paused long enough to pat Barney's head, and the dog rewarded him by tagging along, woofing excitedly now and again. When the doorbell failed to get a response, Lee pounded on the door and called Liza's name. After several unsuccessful tries, he gave up and started to leave.

The door jerked wide, and Liza stood there, her long, sleep-tousled hair falling about her shoulders as she tied the belt of her robe.

He pushed past her without invitation, demanding, "Where did you go?"

Something very like relief touched her face before Liza yawned and asked, "Why do you care?"

"Why?" he repeated in disbelief. "You ran away last evening acting like some kind of crazy woman. I spent half the night trying to find you."

"It wasn't work hours."

Lee grabbed her shoulders. "Stop it, Liza. I was worried." Exasperation tinged his voice. "Were you with Evans?"

She jerked away. "Who appointed you my keeper?"

Each assessed the other's antagonism. "You need one."

"Get out."

Lee remained where he stood. "Not until you tell me where you were."

"Like I said before, it's not your concern." She pointed to the door. "Good-bye."

"If you don't tell me, I'll contact Evans. He'll enlighten me."

A smile touched her face. "I doubt he'd tell you anything."

"Liza, I'm warning you," Lee muttered. "I'll turn you over my knee like your parents should have done."

"Don't come into my parents' home, criticizing the way they raised me. Yours didn't do such a great job either, Lee Hayden."

Unable to look at her, he glanced at the plaque hanging on the entry-hall wall. " 'Be ye angry, and sin not: let not the sun go down upon your wrath,' " he read, and was filled with remorse. He knew they both spoke out of emotion, neither giving much thought to their retaliatory verbal warfare. "I'm sorry."

"Me, too," she admitted.

"I owe you an apology. I shouldn't have sprung the news on you like that. I called last night, and when I didn't get an answer, I thought you might do something you'd regret."

"You didn't push me into doing anything disastrous. I did spend the night with Rick. . . . But it's not what you think," she explained hurriedly. "My parents were involved in a serious accident. He took me to the hospital."

"Liza, I'm sorry. Are they okay?"

"The doctor said everything looked good early this morning. I've talked with both of them. Daddy had a heart attack. Mama only regained consciousness shortly before I left. Now, if you'll excuse me, I have lots to do before I go back to the hospital."

"Can I drive you to the hospital?"

"It would be simpler if I drove myself."

"In what?" he asked, reminding her of the damage to her vehicle.

"Mom's car is here. They drove Daddy's truck."

"You're tired. Let me take you," Lee

requested. "What else can I do to help out?"

"Dave and Rick will be over later to take care of things," she said. "That's how neighbors are here in the country."

"How long before you're ready to go?"

"Around eight."

"I'll be back." She nodded and closed the door. Lee kept walking but patted Barney's head when the animal tried to engage him in play. He opened the car door and sat down, all the while considering the shock Liza must have experienced last night when she learned of her parents' accident. That news coming on top of the damage to her car and the bomb he'd dropped on her must have been devastating.

Starting the car, Lee vowed to be a better friend. She probably wasn't going to be receptive to his efforts to help, but help he would. He owed her that much.

Liza's thoughts ran rampant with Lee's behavior and her feelings for him. How could she be hurt and angry one moment, and forgiving the next? "Don't be stupid; you'd forgive him anything."

The bell rang. He showed up right on time. She came down the stairs slowly. Opening the door, Liza invited him inside. She picked up her purse from the table and checked for her house keys, jumping when the phone rang. "Rick," she exclaimed. "I thought the hospital might be calling."

Lee stood nearby, listening to the one-sided conversation. Outwardly he showed no reaction, but he made no effort to give her any privacy.

She turned her back, lowering her voice. "Sure, why not? No, that won't be necessary. Lee came by and offered to drive me in. No, it'll be okay. See you later. Thanks, Rick. Bye." She replaced the receiver.

"Evans?"

"Yes, he's meeting me at the hospital later so he can visit with Mom and Dad, and then he's taking me out to dinner."

"Would you rather he picked you up now?"

Liza's head snapped up. He almost sounded jealous. "I told him you were taking me. If you've changed your mind, I'll drive myself."

"I want to do this for you," he said, taking the small bag she had packed for her parents.

In the car, Lee questioned her about the extent of her parents' injuries. He surprised her further by parking in the lot rather than pulling up at the door. "I thought I'd come in and say hello if you think it's okay?"

"What's your mom's favorite flower?" he asked as they neared the gift shop. "I'd like to do something to cheer her up."

"I suppose it's the least you can do for that comment about my upbringing," Liza told him.

He was back within minutes, carrying a vase of fresh-cut flowers and a single rose, which he handed to Liza. "Once more, I apologize for allowing my mouth to get out of control."

Lee escorted Liza to her mother's room. If possible, her mother's bruising seemed even more vivid today. Several times, Liza saw her wince when she moved the slightest bit.

After a few minutes of watching Lee charm the woman, Liza checked her watch. "I'm going up to see Daddy. Any messages?"

"Give him my love. I talked to him on the phone earlier."

Her father seemed happy to see her, even though he was clearly despondent. "I'd offer you a seat, but they aren't too keen on visitors here. Figure they can keep people from visiting too long by making them stand."

"The short visiting periods are for your benefit, Daddy."

"Liza, what will I do about the crops?"

She laid her hand on his. "We'll manage," she soothed. "Just don't worry about it now. Mom sends her love."

"They won't let me see her. Dr. Mayes said maybe after a couple of days. I'm so tired of this place. I wish they'd leave me alone."

"I bet," Liza countered. "Then you'd be grumbling about the service."

"For what they're charging, I'd be entitled."

His skewed logic brought a grin to her face. "I knew Mom spoiled you, but I had no idea how much until now."

"You're an ungrateful child." He laughed when she started to giggle.

"I'll have you know this ungrateful child called her boss this morning to tell him she'll be out of work indefinitely."

"Are you sure?"

Liza fidgeted beneath the intensity of his stare. "I think it's best. Any idea on what they plan next?"

"They won't say. They're monitoring me with all of this equipment, and the doctor says six weeks, maybe longer, with my leg. The timing couldn't be worse."

Irregular rhythms crossed the monitor screen. "Settle down, Daddy. You know they're trying to determine how severe your attack was."

"I know, but Dr. Mayes won't promise me anything. Said it could be weeks."

"Thank God you've got weeks," Liza whispered when the nurse came over to the bed to check on him and indicated she should go. "See you later." She kissed his cheek and slipped out of the curtained area.

Back in her mother's room, she described the situation and what she had said. "He's not going to settle down until he's reassured that things will work out. When I think about what could have happened to you both, nothing else matters."

Her mother's eyes drifted shut for a moment. "I'll remind him he's aggravating the condition when they let me talk to him again."

"Good idea. Why don't I ask the nurse if she can arrange a phone call? You tell him I fully intend to do the best job I can," Liza said.

"That's all he can ask for."

"I'm sorry this had to happen," Lee said. "I'll be happy to help in every way possible."

Sarah Stephens smiled at him. "Thanks. It's good to know you're there if we need you. Liza has been blessed with a wonderful employer."

He seemed surprised by her mother's comment. "I've got to go. Take care of yourself, Mrs. Stephens. Walk me out, Liza?"

Outside the room, Lee touched her arm. "Call if you need me?"

"Sure," she agreed. "And Lee, I'm sorry for the way I've acted. Forgive me."

"Of course. I should have recognized that you were operating on emotion. Maybe I'll be able to get a good night's sleep tonight. I'd stay longer, but I have plans for this afternoon."

Liza said good-bye and hesitated a moment longer, watching him walk away. "Lee," she called when he was halfway down the hall. "Thanks again for all you did today. It helps Mom and Dad to know I have people I can depend on."

He regarded her for a few seconds. "No problem. Take care."

His kindness played on Liza's mind. She was so confused by his ability to turn his emotions on and off at will. Perhaps being a lawyer made him cold and untouchable at times. That coldness, and the way he could shut her out, hurt more than anything else did. She was saddened even more by the fact that their comfortable friendship might be destroyed because of her growing attraction.

He stopped and turned back. "Liza? Did you really call Uncle John this morning?"

She nodded.

"Why didn't you call me?"

"Because I didn't think you'd understand what I had to do."

He took a few steps forward. "How could you think that? I know you have to be with your parents."

"It's not just for now, Lee," she explained. "I may have to resign. At best, I probably won't be back to work until the fall."

Liza gave him full marks for restraining himself as obviously genuine astonishment changed his expression.

"Let me know how things are going with you. I do care, you know."

Liza prayed he did.

CHAPTER 6

Rick arrived shortly after Lee's departure, giving Liza no time to worry about Lee's lack of reaction to her plans. Her mother and Rick caught up on the news, and Mom told him he should visit his family more often. At seven, she insisted they go meet Kitty and Dave for dinner.

Liza hesitated, but she knew there wasn't much she could do for her mother or father.

They went to a local pizza restaurant. Red dominated the room, from the countertops to the checkered tablecloths. Candle containers vied with red pepper flakes and Parmesan cheese in shaker bottles, table ads, and menus in small jackets.

Kitty and Dave shared a booth and seemed oblivious to their arrival.

"Cut it out, you two lovebirds." Rick grinned at Liza when they jumped apart.

"Liza!" Kitty cried, slipping from the booth to hug her. "How are your parents?

111

I'm so sorry."

"Better. Daddy's not enjoying his stay. Mom will be better when they let her see him for herself. Her mothering instincts seem unaffected. She just felt well enough to tell Rick he should visit more often."

"Must be a mother thing," Rick said. "Mom tells me that all the time."

Everyone laughed, and Rick indicated Liza should slip into the booth. Kitty slid back in beside Dave.

"It was so frightening," Kitty said.

"You're telling me. I thought the officer came to tell me about my car."

"This hasn't been your weekend. The news shocked everyone."

"I called Mr. Wilson to let him know I'll be out awhile."

"Does Lee know?"

Kitty knew about Lee's reaction to her last request for time off. Neither understood his strong reaction.

"Yes," Liza said, not really wanting to get into it with Rick and Dave looking on.

"And?"

Liza glanced at the men, then back at Kitty. Reaching for the tea pitcher, she filled Rick's glass and then her own. "He didn't have a lot to say. Tell me about the party. What happened after I left?"

Smiles wreathed all three faces. "Well, there was some big to-do when a certain man got down on bended knee and asked a certain woman to marry him," Kitty said.

Puzzlement soon gave way to understanding as Liza realized they were the mystery couple. "Oh, I missed your proposal? What did he do?" She looked from one to the other and demanded, "Did you really ask her in front of everyone?"

"He did," Kitty said. "I was so shocked. He brought me a bowl of homemade strawberry ice cream, and the first thing I saw was this sparkling in the center." She held out her hand to show her new diamond.

"She never did eat that ice cream," Dave said. "Perfectly good waste of some of the best ice cream ever made."

Kitty tapped his arm. "Then he bravely knelt and asked me to marry him."

Dave sat a little taller in his seat at Kitty's mention of bravery as the waitress slid two piping hot pizzas onto the table.

"We ordered," Kitty explained, passing around the plates. "Dave thought you might be hungry."

"We certainly ate here enough in the past for you to know what I like."

The feeling of being watched was strong. Liza glanced up to find Lee near the doorway. She waved at him, and he returned the greeting. He looked tired. A wave of guilt coursed through Liza.

Kitty spotted him at the same time. "There's Lee. Let's invite him to join us."

"I don't know. Liza might . . . ," Rick began.

"It's okay," she said softly. "I'll ask."

Rick stood, and she scooted past him, unaware of the curious looks her friends shared. Liza walked over to the little corner table where Lee sat. "Hi. We thought you might like to join us."

He smiled at her. "No thanks. I don't want to interrupt your date."

"It's not a date, just old friends having dinner together. Kit and Dave are talking about their engagement."

"I didn't realize they got engaged."

Liza traced one finger about the checkerboard pattern of the cloth. "Last night. It sounds like we missed some production."

He pushed back the wooden chair. "I'll walk over with you and congratulate them."

She was very aware of his hand resting in the small of her back as they walked over to the booth. Rick stood, and Liza slipped into her seat.

"Pull up a chair," Kitty invited.

Lee shook his head. "I won't crash your

party. Liza just told me the news. I wanted to congratulate you both."

"Nonsense," Dave said. "The more the merrier. Sit down."

They kept insisting, so Lee finally borrowed a chair from a nearby table and sat down. The waitress took his order for a soft drink and Kitty's request for another plate.

Kitty grabbed his hand. "Let's say grace. Our pizzas are getting cold."

He appeared surprised by her action but accepted Rick's hand and bowed his head as she prayed. Kit took on the job of serving the food, and soon everyone had a couple of slices.

The conversation was as varied as the table's occupants until Kitty started talking about planning a fall wedding. "It's the only time I'll be able to get my future husband out of town for a honeymoon. I want you to be my maid of honor," she told Liza. "And Rick will be Dave's best man."

"You should ask Dad," Rick said.

"I did. He said he'd rather you did it," Dave said. "You know how he hates to wear a tux."

Rick grimaced playfully. "I hoped you'd choose bib overalls and caps."

Liza giggled at Kitty's expression.

"No way."

"You are asking a bit much of a country boy. I felt sure you were planning the nature thing down by the pond — shorts, bare feet, and daisies in your hair."

"Stop joking. We're having a lovely wedding with everyone beautifully dressed."

"If you plan this shindig soon enough, I should be able to attend before my next job starts up."

"Believe me, she's already checking your itinerary for this visit," Dave told his brother.

Kitty looked at Lee. "And, of course, you have a standing invitation."

"Thanks."

Liza dropped the pizza crust onto her plate. "I'd have given a nickel to see Dave on bended knee."

"What happened to you anyway?" Kit asked. "I looked all over. I wanted to show you my ring."

"I went home." Liza refused to look in Lee's direction.

"Wow, good thing you went. You must have had a feeling something wasn't right."

The something not right had started at the party and worsened by the time she got home. Tears dampened Liza's eyes. "The news took years off my life."

She glanced up when Rick gently squeezed

her fingers and caught Lee's gaze on them. "Don't worry," he comforted. "God is in control."

"There's no other way I could make it through this."

Kitty changed the subject. Rick brought them up to date on what he'd been doing, telling them about London.

"I'd love to go there one day," Kitty said wistfully.

"It's very different from here," Rick said.

The evening passed quickly. All too soon, it was time to say good night.

"This has been fun, but I need to get home. Ready, Liza?"

"She can ride with us," Kit said. "I'm spending the night at her place anyway."

"I'd be happy to take Liza home," Lee offered.

Everyone looked to her for a decision. "I can ride with Lee. We need to talk anyway. Thanks for everything, Rick."

He kissed her cheek and slipped from the booth. "I'll be in touch."

"I appreciate the help. Once we know what's going on with Daddy, I'll know better what to do."

"Take care. I'll check with you tomorrow."

Liza nodded. Emotion clogged her throat as the obvious love of her friends surrounded her. She wasn't alone. Not only was God with her every step of the way, He had sent these wonderful people to help carry her load.

Lee insisted on picking up the check for their celebratory dinner, and after he paid, they walked out to the parking lot.

"I'll meet you at the house before too late," Kitty promised. "My clothes are in the car."

Liza hugged her friend. "Thanks, Kit." Lee opened the car door and waited for her to get in. "Thanks for taking me home. I wanted to talk to you about this morning."

Lee didn't start the car right away. He turned to face her, resting one arm on the steering wheel. "My behavior was totally uncalled for. I had no right to strike out at you like that."

Liza felt the urge to take the conversation further and discuss the information he'd sprung on her, but now wasn't the time. Her emotions were still pretty raw. It hurt to think that Mr. Wilson hadn't shared the news himself.

"Let's forget it happened," she suggested.

Lee wanted nothing more than to forget, but he knew he owed Liza an explanation.

"Don't blame Uncle John. I'm the reason

we didn't tell you."

"When did he start thinking about retirement? Mr. Wilson's not that old, and he's never mentioned it before."

"He and Aunt Clara want to travel. I suppose he plans to maintain a certain degree of control, but I'd be responsible for day-to-day operations."

"I see."

Did she? He wasn't so sure Liza was convinced. "He wants me to be certain I want to live here before I commit to taking over. I'm beginning to feel at home. I like the people. Can't promise I'll lose all my big-city ways at once, though."

When she nodded, not saying anything else, Lee wondered about Liza's reaction. "Friends?"

"Sure."

Lee found the conversation less stilted on the way home. When Lee drove into the yard, Barney greeted them by barking as he jumped up on the side of the car.

Horrified, Liza reached through the window and pushed the dog away. "Barney, get down. Bad dog."

Lee smiled when she started digging in her purse for the house key. How she got so much stuff in that small bag intrigued him. The keys jangled as she pulled them out.

"Thanks again, Lee."

"Let me walk you to the door."

"That's okay. Barney's right here. I doubt there's anyone waiting in the shadows with him running around, barking like that."

Lee eyed the dog. "True. Liza," he began hesitantly. "I hope you understand I only want what's best for you." He understood she was on an emotional tightrope when it took her a few seconds to manage more than a nod.

"I don't know what I'd do without my friends. The Lord has truly blessed me."

Taken aback, Lee wondered why she didn't feel angry at God for all that had happened to her this weekend. "You believe that, don't you? Despite the fact that your parents are both in the hospital, you feel blessed?"

"I only have to look for blessings to find them," Liza said. "My parents could have died in that crash. For that matter, Daddy could have died out there, in a field by himself, because we didn't know he had a heart problem. I could be alone, not knowing where to turn next. Instead, I have wonderful friends and neighbors who are pulling together and helping me do what needs to be done. Yes, I feel wonderfully blessed. I have many reasons to praise the

Lord today and every day."

Lee hoped the car's interior light didn't illuminate his discomfort as Liza continued to speak of her faith.

"I'm never alone. God is with me always and has been since the day I asked Him into my heart. Most of all, I'm amazed that He loves me despite my failings. And believe me, I have plenty. His grace is worth more than anything to me."

"You'd better get inside. Tomorrow's another busy day."

"I hope we can talk about this more in the future, Lee."

Resigned that she saw through his delaying tactic, he said, "I'm sure we will."

A couple of hours later, Liza and Kit sat at the kitchen table, drinking cocoa and discussing how their lives had changed in one weekend.

"And to think you were saying he didn't have a ring on your finger just minutes before the party," Liza teased after examining the round diamond more closely. "This thing is huge." She grinned as she pretended Kit's hand weighed a ton.

Kit's laughter was pure joy. "I know. The truth is, I've wanted him to ask me forever. I guess I used false bravado to cover my fear that he wouldn't."

"I never doubted he'd ask. Dave has loved you forever. You realize what you've agreed to, don't you?"

Kit shrugged. "Sharing my life with the man I love?"

"And sharing his life," Liza reminded. "Have you considered what that means?"

"It'll take some adjusting, but we'll work things out."

"Dave is a farmer, Kit. He doesn't have nine-to-five hours. Granted, you'll see more of him once you're living in the same house, but the land places all sorts of demands on those who choose to care for it."

A smile touched her friend's lips. "I'll be the one thing I said I'd never be — a farmer's wife. Goes to show the mind can't control the heart when it comes to love."

Amen, Liza thought. How could she possibly be in love with a man who couldn't understand her choices? "Mama always says, 'Never say never.' "

"What about Lee? What really happened last night?"

Reconciled to the truth of the matter, Liza admitted, "Mostly I made an idiot of myself."

Kit set the mug on the table. "How?"

"I was feeling flattered when he showed

me a bit of attention." Embarrassed, she forced herself to continue. "I took offense to something he said. We argued, then he dropped this bomb on me about how Mr. Wilson is talking about retirement and he's going to take over. I was devastated. He explained that Mr. Wilson is waiting on his decision. It hurts, though. After all the years I've given that office, I expected a certain amount of loyalty. They should have at least told me what they're planning. It changes everything."

"In what way?"

"Mr. Wilson and I understand each other. His working style is nothing like Lee's."

"Understandable. Younger man. Has more to prove. Would you leave the firm?"

Would she? Liza didn't know. She'd never considered not working for Mr. Wilson. Could she work with Lee, given their problems? "I honestly don't know."

"How do you feel about Lee?"

"I'm so confused by his behavior. Most of the time, I feel like an office fixture."

"So you think Lee doesn't see you as a woman?" Kitty asked.

Liza shrugged as she stood and took their cups over to the sink. She rinsed them quickly and placed them in the dishwasher. "I don't know what to think. Lee's like the weather. Wait a moment, and he changes. I thought we were becoming friends, but now I feel like a body who keeps the office running efficiently."

"That bothers you?"

"A lot," Liza admitted, almost reluctantly. "I don't want to be attracted to him. He doesn't understand me at all. He doesn't attend church, and I've never met anyone more focused on himself."

"But you've developed a short circuit between your heart and your brain?"

Liza laughed out loud at Kit's analogy. "System overload. That's me."

"What are you going to do?"

"Nothing. Well, actually I'm dropping the load right into God's hands. He's more capable of sorting this out than I am."

"Good idea. There's a reason you came into Lee's life, and only time will bring an answer."

"A lot of prayer won't go amiss either," Liza said pointedly.

"We'll pray without ceasing," Kit vowed, smiling at her friend as they started up the stairs.

CHAPTER 7

The pattern for the remainder of her summer fell into place over the next few days. By Friday, they knew nothing less than bypass surgery could correct her father's heart problem, and it was scheduled for early Monday morning.

Liza felt even more frightened when the doctor outlined the procedure, which involved opening his chest from top to bottom and stripping veins from his good leg to use to repair the damaged vessels.

The doctors allowed Liza's mother to accompany her to the CCU when they gave Dad the diagnosis. He didn't take the news well, but Liza suspected he controlled his outrage in her mother's presence. As always, his wife's influence soothed him, and he relegated his health to secondary importance when he saw her.

A cold knot of fear formed in her stomach as Liza watched them, considering the impact of the responsibility the situation placed upon her shoulders.

An efficient nurse whisked her mother away at the first sign of tiredness, leaving her father's attention focused on his present problem. When the nurse came in with more medication, he demanded they stop drugging him so he could talk to his daughter.

"No manager for the farm," he declared.

Liza sat still, her arms stiffening as she pressed her hands against her knees to fortify herself. "But, Daddy —"

"You can do just as good a job, better in my opinion," he said before she could finish the sentence.

She prayed her despair wasn't obvious to him. He didn't need the added worry of an incompetent being responsible for his livelihood. "I hope I don't let you down."

"Liza, baby, I'll be as close as the house, and all our friends are willing to help. The pastor came by this afternoon. He said they're putting together a schedule to help."

But wanting and doing are different things, Liza thought. All those good intentions wouldn't be much help if the people didn't carry through. What would happen when they got caught up in the demands of their own farms? And given how busy every farmer got this time of year, they would be borrowing from Peter to pay Paul. She grimaced at the pun.

"Besides, your mother will be home soon."

"Lot of good she'll be with you sick," Liza countered with a knowing smile.

"I have enough confidence in you for the both of us," he told her without so much as a blink of an eye.

Let's hope it's justified, Liza thought as she agreed to take on the farm.

Even the worst days at the office didn't compare with the juggling act Liza endured over the next three weeks.

Released on the day of her husband's surgery, Sarah Stephens insisted on going straight to the waiting area. Nothing Liza said could convince her otherwise. Her mother remained at the hospital after her father moved from the CCU to a room. Liza drove back and forth to check on them and bring her mother fresh clothes until they released him on Thursday.

Ecstatic over having him home, Liza thought they were through the worst of things . . . until he developed complications from a cold that resulted in his returning to the hospital for another brief stay.

Liza listened carefully when seasoned

farmers took her under their wings and taught her how to deal with the situations that arose. The major surgery left her father in a weakened state, and she dared not say anything that would add to his stress.

Exhausted both emotionally and physically, Liza refused to look beyond each day. Rick helped all he could, and Mr. Wilson called to check on her parents and reassure her that they would make do until her return. She disliked the idea of leaving them in a bind, but the options were limited.

On Thursday night Lee came by to bring what was left of a formerly gorgeous fern. "We tried," he said with a shrug. "Evidently neither of us has your green thumb."

Liza took the hanger, grimacing as she fondled the brown-tipped fronds. "Didn't you water it, or talk to it, or anything?"

Lee laughed. "We watered it. Actually it got so much water, I'm surprised it didn't learn to swim. As for talking, I doubt the clients would approve."

"Poor, lonely, drowned plant," Liza crooned, setting it on the corner of the porch. "Other than this, how are things going?"

"Don't ask." Lee adjusted his pantleg as he sat and made himself comfortable beside her in the swing. "The files and your desk are in shambles. Everything is stacked to the ceiling, and of course every folder I need is in the stack to be filed. It takes forever to find something."

"And it never occurred to you to file them?"

He ignored her question. "When are you coming back?"

She stirred uneasily. "I have no idea."

Lee's gaze narrowed, a heavy frown weighing down his face. "What kind of answer is that?"

His query destroyed their earlier ease. The tension grew as he sat, glaring and waiting.

"The only one I can give you," she said with quiet emphasis, glancing toward the house. "I'm needed here."

"I need you at the office, too. I can't do this alone."

"I can't help you right now. You'll do just fine."

"You don't understand. All my life I've been an overachiever. The highest grades, the highest SAT scores, the finest college.

"Please don't think I'm bragging, but I was recruited by a number of prestigious firms. I missed home and jumped at the chance to join a larger firm in Charlotte. I was certain I'd make partner in record time."

"What happened?"

"I realized I'm not a team player. At first, I tried to do whatever it took to assure I was in line for advancement. But my integrity is too important to me. I took on some pro bono cases they assigned, then I found out they didn't plan on me giving the same attention to detail to those clients as I did the ones with billable hours. It wasn't like they were bankrupting themselves by giving away a few hours of legal service. I refused to give the cases less than they deserved. The senior partners weren't very happy with me. I can't go back to that kind of law again."

Lee knew he wasn't being fair to Liza, but he needed her desperately.

"You won't have to," she pointed out. "Evidently Mr. Wilson is comfortable enough with you being there to go off on extended vacations."

"What about your priorities, Liza? You love your job far more than you do this farm."

"And I love my parents far more than either my job or the farm. I have other obligations, more important priorities right now. My parents and their livelihood come before my own needs. Why did you come here tonight? You knew my decision."

Lee all but jumped from the swing. "I thought you'd be back once you got things under control. Obviously I was wrong."

"Obviously."

He walked away without another word, Barney's barking echoing his departure.

Lee's comment about her priorities made Liza realize the need to update Mr. Wilson on her plans. She wished she could make Lee understand: While she preferred the security of the office to the strangeness of the farm, she had no choice. If only she could turn back the clock.

She set aside the following morning to see Mr. Wilson. She could take care of it while her parents went for their follow-up visits with the doctor.

Family responsibility wasn't an alien concept to Mr. Wilson, Liza told herself the next morning as she unlocked the office door and stepped inside. The office was exactly as Lee described — a disaster area as well as very empty. The answering machine blinked repeatedly with a number of messages awaiting return calls.

Liza set her purse on the desktop and reached for the phone. She called the temp who usually filled in for her to ask if she was available for an indefinite time. The woman seemed eager, and Liza told her she'd be back in touch as soon as she got approval from Mr. Wilson.

While she waited, Liza slipped into the routine of her job. She wrote out message slips, opened several days' mail, checked folders, and filed those she could. She made notes on others, then stacked them in orderly piles on Lee's and Mr. Wilson's desks. It seemed she'd been away for only a day or so as she read the notes both men had left for her. 'Do this.' 'Remind me.' A despondent smile crossed her face as she updated the appointments on the computer. She would miss her job.

The bong of the grandfather clock in the corner confirmed the hour. Liza grabbed her purse and glanced around one last time. Just as she reached the door, Mr. Wilson pushed it wide, the warmth of his smile echoing in his voice as he welcomed her. "Liza, are you back with us?"

She shook her head regretfully. "Afraid not. I needed to talk to you. I did a bit of work while I waited."

He nodded approvingly. "As efficient as ever. Come into my office."

Liza followed, taking the seat across from

his desk. She answered his questions concerning her parents and blinked back hot tears. "It looks like I'm going to have to request an indefinite leave of absence, sir. Daddy will be out of commission for the rest of the summer . . . maybe longer."

In the manner Liza expected, John Wilson sat, silently analyzing her words. He smiled at her as if she were a small child, his kindly words bringing relief to her troubled emotions. "I'm sure it's the only way. Of course, we hate to lose you for any length of time."

"I hate to go," she admitted, "but Daddy's not content with anyone else supervising."

"You'll have to be patient and understanding," he advised. "This is hard for all of you, but it's particularly difficult for Paul."

"The surgery left him weak as a kitten, and his leg is giving him a great deal of pain."

Mr. Wilson rose and came around the desk to pass her a tissue. "I'm sure it'll work itself out. How long do you need?"

Her forehead creased. "I'm not sure. Right now I'm thinking three months, until Daddy's back on his feet."

"Your job will still be here after that time, and longer if need be. We can hire someone on a temporary basis."

"Thank you, sir," Liza said. "You don't know what a load off my shoulders this is. Lee's upset that I haven't made the office my priority lately."

"Lee doesn't understand," his uncle explained. "I doubt he's ever experienced what you're going through now. Things would certainly be different if he were facing similar circumstances."

"I pray he never has to," Liza said.

"Amen to that. I'm going to continue your salary, Liza."

"You don't have to do that," she protested.

"Consider it a bonus. You've been my right hand for years."

They discussed her plan to get the temp in, and he asked Liza to handle a few tasks for him before she left. She sorted out the minor details before leaving the office.

As she walked across the parking lot, Liza relaxed for the first time in days. Her parents were going to be okay. Mr. Wilson had accepted her decision, and with everything else falling in place, the thought of managing the farm didn't frighten her as much.

The day seemed perfect — the warmth, the blueness of the sky, and the smiling faces of the people she met. She returned the greetings, carefully noting the messages people asked her to deliver to her folks.

She didn't see Lee until he walked up beside her. "What brings you to our part of town?"

Liza jerked around. "I was talking to Mr. Wilson. You told me to get my priorities in order."

"True, but I'd hoped you would choose us."

"I don't have a choice here," she protested, almost pleading with him to understand. "I've prayed about this, and I'm led to do what needs to be done. These are my parents."

"And where do you come into all this?"

"Everywhere. Nowhere. I don't know," Liza said. "It's all so confusing."

"And unfair," Lee added.

"I suppose it is unfair that an active man has to be sick during one of the busiest times of the year. Do you think that's what Daddy wants?"

"But what about you? How can you be so self-sacrificing?"

How could she make him understand? "It's not sacrifice to help those you love."

"What about your life? What you love? You don't want to farm. If you did, you'd never have dedicated the time to becoming a paralegal. You did that for you."

"What is this really about, Lee? Why are you so convinced I'm giving . . ." Her words trailed off as another realization hit her. "You know, I thought your objections had to do with me leaving the office in a bind, but there's something else. Something I can't quite put my finger on."

His expression attempted to belie her words. "Why would you say that?"

"You're a 'me' type person, Lee. I'm not saying it's a bad thing, but there's a time when self ceases to be important. Tell me you wouldn't do the same if this involved your parents."

"They understand I have a career."

Liza's eyes widened. "You'd put career before the people who brought you into the world?"

"Not exactly. But they wouldn't ask. My parents are very self-sufficient. They've never asked anything of me."

"Mine didn't ask either. I made the decision. And just maybe your parents should ask something of you. It might help you understand what I've got to do."

"I'm not going to argue with you. I think they're wrong to let you throw your life away with both hands."

"Maybe you're wrong, Lee. Have you considered that? I've got to go. Mom and

Dad are waiting at the doctor's office. Bye."

Liza was trembling when she settled in the car and pulled the door closed. She had never realized the depth of Lee's self-absorption until this moment. Surely he knew what the Bible said about honoring your parents. This went beyond honor for her. It was love for the people who had given her life and breath. It had nothing to do with guilt, but everything to do with her saying thank you. If Lee didn't understand, too bad. She wasn't going to let him change her mind.

It's a battle I'm not going to win, Lee thought as he closed the office door behind him. Liza's conviction outweighed his arguments every time. In his heart, Lee knew she had no choice. It did bug him that she wouldn't be around to help him. Instead, he'd have to muddle along on his own.

He stuck his head into his uncle's office to let him know he was back from the courthouse.

"Got a minute?"

Lee crossed the expanse of the expensive Oriental rug and sprawled in one of the chairs across from the desk. "What's up?"

"Liza came by."

"I saw her out in the parking lot. Looks

like she's prioritized us right out of her life."

John Wilson kicked back in his burgundy leather chair and eyed Lee. "What other choice does she have?"

"Surely her dad could get someone to help out," Lee said. "It's not fair to Liza."

"Son, there's a lot you don't understand about family responsibility."

Lee shrugged. "You're right. I don't understand."

John Wilson propped his chin on his fingertips and eyed Lee. "Are you worried about her or yourself?"

"Both of us. We make a good team. She's been a lot of help to me."

"Then give her the support she needs now. You're an only child, and the day may come when you're forced to set aside your life to care for aging parents."

"Dad's shared his plans to provide care for their senior years."

"The haves and the have-nots," his uncle said. "The Stephenses don't have that kind of money. They're working-class people who depend on that farm for their livelihood. Paul Stephens doesn't know anything but the land.

"And if you knew anything about Liza, you'd know she's struggling with this decision. She's the most dedicated employee

I've ever had, and frankly I'm willing to limp along without her for a while rather than risk losing her completely."

Lee felt like a thoroughly chastened little boy. He might as well reveal the rest of his role in this situation. "I don't suppose she asked you about me taking over the firm?"

His uncle's chair shot up straight. "I thought we agreed not to tell her until after we finalized things."

He nodded, sharing the grim news. "We did. And that was my intent until I let my emotions take control of my tongue and blabbed. I tried to explain, but I'm not sure she accepts my apologies."

"You'd do well to treat that girl right," John advised. "Losing her would be the worst thing that could happen to this office."

And me, Lee thought. "What do you suppose it is about us? She frustrates me faster than anyone I know. It starts out innocently enough. I ask a question, and she gives me the answer I don't want to hear. Next thing I know, the situation escalates into an argument."

"Are you attracted to her?"

Was he? Lee found it difficult to define exactly how he felt about Liza. "She's a beautiful woman inside and out."

John nodded agreement. "She is. Always has been — even before she lost all that weight. She's got the sweetest spirit. If Clara and I had a daughter, I'd want her to be just like Liza. Perhaps you're disappointed because you can't see her every day?"

"Perhaps." Lee pushed himself from the chair. "Guess I'd better start sorting through the mail."

"Liza's already taken care of that. She worked while she waited to talk to me."

Lee felt almost relieved.

"The temp will be in tomorrow. Rhonda has a different working style than our Liza," his uncle warned. "Don't expect miracles."

"I'm missing Liza already."

CHAPTER 8

Much to Liza's dismay, the confrontation with Lee stayed on her mind. The lengthy periods when she had time to think were definitely a negative of farm work. She knew Kit and Dave would string her up if she didn't attend their engagement party tonight. Without a doubt, Lee would be there. Hopefully they wouldn't argue again. What a mess.

Liza's friends had banded together to help her retain her sanity. Rick had been a daily blessing, and in the beginning she depended heavily on him. He explained things she couldn't to her dad and cheered her on as her confidence level increased. It hadn't taken long to gain the self-assurance she needed to get the job done. She attributed the change to all the prayers being offered up on her behalf.

Excited about the party, Kitty called several times to remind Liza and just to chat about what they would wear. Liza planned to use the outing as an excuse to dress up.

The strain and worry served one positive purpose — that of getting her over her plateau. Those first few days of not having her mom around to insist she eat did the trick. While running back and forth to the hospital, Liza frequently made do with little or nothing at night. Her last ten pounds and five more were gone, and she felt pleased that she had met her goal.

The accident brought about a number of changes in the Stephenses' home. When she started dieting, her mother became her biggest opponent, arguing she didn't need to lose weight. Then she claimed Liza lost too much weight and concentrated on fattening her up.

Now Sarah Stephens asked for her daughter's help. The heart attack frightened her mother into accepting that healthy eating was as necessary as breathing. Her father complained about the tasteless food and lack of things he loved, like homemade biscuits and gravy, but the changed eating habits helped everyone.

After combing her hair up into an elegant chignon, Liza removed the pale pink sheath from the hanger and pulled it on. The dress skimmed her body, stopping at her knees.

The color complemented the tan she'd gained as a result of spending more time outside. Slipping on her sandals, Liza looked in the mirror and gave her hair one final pat.

Rick's eyes widened appreciatively when she answered the door, and his wolf whistle made her laugh. "Hello, gorgeous."

"I didn't think you'd notice."

"How could I not?"

"It's the first time I've been out since the accident, and I intend to celebrate."

Rick grinned.

Liza walked over to kiss her mother good night. "You have a nice visit with Granny and Aunt Mary," she ordered. "And get to bed early. You've had a stressful day."

"Yes, ma'am." Her mother winked. "Have a good time, honey."

"Night, Granny, Aunt Mary. Make sure she minds you." Liza squeezed her mother's hand gently.

"If she does, it'll be a first," said Granny. "You look pretty."

"Thanks."

Her father smiled at her from the recliner. "I'm not sure I should let you out of the house in that get-up."

"Your little girl is all grown up." Liza kissed his cheek.

Family and friends of the couple filled the country club's restaurant. Liza waved at several people as she made her way over to where Kit and Dave were receiving their guests.

"Well, look at you," Kitty said. "Don't you know you're not supposed to outshine the bride-to-be?"

"What? This old thing is nothing compared to those stars in your eyes," Liza teased in return.

Kitty giggled, and Liza joined in.

They were complete opposites, both in looks and personalities. Kitty was fair-haired and vibrant, where Liza was dark and subdued. It always amazed Liza that they were best friends, the closest thing to sisters.

Over the years, Liza had become used to being dragged along to various events as one of the town's eligible young women. Kitty never hesitated to get Liza an invitation along with her own, and they made up the numbers more times than Liza cared to admit. Thanks to her friend, she'd had more than her fair share of party invitations and blind dates, few of which she'd been thrilled over.

Of course, tonight was a different story. What would she do once Kit was married? It would never be the same again.

Liza moved on down the line, hugging Dave and then Kit's parents. "You're looking mighty handsome," she told Jason.

"And you're stunning."

Dave's parents were next in the line. "I'm so happy for them," she told his mother.

Mrs. Evans smiled at her son. "It's about time. I want grandchildren before I'm too old to enjoy them."

Liza and Kit had never discussed children. She assumed they would have a family, but probably not right away. Hopefully Mrs. Evans wouldn't start pushing the newlyweds. No doubt Kit would stand her ground. Her outspoken friend wouldn't be pushed into anything before she was ready.

"How are your parents?" Mrs. Evans asked.

"Doing better. Granny and Aunt Mary are visiting tonight. Daddy's chafing at the restraints, but we're pleased with his progress."

"I can imagine," Mrs. Evans agreed. "Liza, can we borrow Rick for a while? He really should be in the receiving line. So many people are asking after him."

"Mom, don't be rude."

The woman looked shocked. "I didn't mean . . . I just thought . . ."

"She's right," Liza said quickly. "I'm sure

everyone is eager to say hello. No sense in them having to chase you down to do it. I'll catch up with you later."

"Traitor," Rick whispered.

"Hey, I'm the queen of family responsibility," she mocked, grinning broadly before she walked away.

Liza paused underneath the ceiling fan to appreciate the cool breeze. It was warm inside tonight. Hopefully the predicted thunderstorm would wait until after Kitty and Dave's guests made it back home.

"Liza."

She turned, searching the crowd.

Jason motioned her over. "Here's a guy who needs some legal advice."

The group of people standing in front of the couple blocked her view. Liza smiled, gesturing that she'd be there in a moment. Despite her earlier anxiety, a thrill of anticipation touched her when she spotted Lee standing next to Jason.

"Hello, Lee."

"Hi. Liza knows paralegals don't give advice, Jason. She could get into serious trouble."

Jason laughed and winked at her. "But she gives good advice."

"What did you want to know?"

Lee's eyebrow rose a fraction. He started

to speak, then stopped himself.

"Tell him how many years you get for not enjoying yourself at a Berenson party."

Liza shifted her gaze to meet Lee's penetrating, pale blue gaze. "Ten years to life as a social outcast."

Jason laughed, clapping Lee on the shoulder. "Hey, it's a joke. You didn't think we were serious?"

Lee appeared to relax, a slightly sheepish smile creeping over his face. "You had me going there for a minute. I wondered how long she'd been advising people."

"I've never started," Liza assured. "I play along because Jason gets such a kick out of the joke."

"And I only use it on lawyers," Jason said. "Got to go. Judy's either planning a career switch to a contortionist or motioning me over. Catch you later."

An uncomfortable silence hovered. "You look good," Lee said.

"Thanks. One of the pluses of worry is weight loss."

"You've caught the attention of more than one person tonight."

Liza shrugged. "The metamorphosis."

"Just how much did you change?"

"Around a hundred pounds."

His mouth dropped open. "You're kidding."

"Not at all. Ask anyone here. Most of them told me I'd be a pretty girl if I'd lose the weight."

"That's cruel."

"I was used to it. My real friends didn't mind."

Liza wondered how Lee would have reacted if he'd known her then. Thanks to her mother's efforts to grow the tiny daughter who had entered the world prematurely, she'd been overweight for as long as she could remember. She'd quickly turned into a chubby toddler. Her weight increased with each of her school years until it stabilized in her twenties. Last year, after the doctor started talking about high blood pressure and cholesterol problems, she'd taken a long look at herself and decided she didn't like what she saw.

"Looks like that line is dwindling. We should find our table," Lee commented.

They moved around the room, reading place cards. She was shocked to find herself seated with Lee. Kitty's doing, no doubt. Where had they put Rick? She glanced at the card on the opposite side. Not there.

Lee pulled out her chair. "I'm glad they seated us together. I don't know that many

148

people in town."

"You and Jason seem rather friendly."

"We've run into each other a few times. We eat lunch at the same restaurant on occasion."

"He's a great guy."

"You're in my seat."

They looked up at Rick.

Lee indicated his name on the card. "No idea where they seated you, but it wasn't here."

"Come on, Liza," Rick said, reaching for her hand. "There's obviously some sort of mix-up."

"I'm here, too, Rick." She pointed to her card.

His mouth thinned with displeasure. "This is crazy. Why wouldn't they seat us together?"

Jason stood at the main table, calling for everyone's attention. "I don't know, but things are about to get underway. You need to find your seat."

"Looks like there's a chair up there," Lee pointed out. "I imagine they saved you a seat with the family."

"Keep out of it, Hayden. Liza's with me."

Lee stood his ground, not wavering when he said, "She's seated at this table. Unless you plan to toss someone out of his seat up there, I don't see anywhere for her to sit."

Liza looked from one to the other. Their antagonism surprised her. This was ridiculous. Surely they weren't fighting over her. "Stop it," she ordered. "I don't believe you two."

"But, Liza . . ."

"Excuse us." She laid a hand on Rick's arm and gestured to the side of the room.

"What's going on?" he demanded.

"I have no idea, but this is Kitty and Dave's night. Please, don't make a scene."

"Why would they seat us separately? They knew I was picking you up."

"I'm sure they wanted all the family together. I'll find you right after dinner," Liza promised.

Rick walked away without another word, and she watched him find his seat at the front table before moving back to her chair. Matchmaker was written all over the seating arrangements. Rick had been placed next to a single woman closer to his age — no doubt someone his mother hoped would entice him home. Liza settled in her chair, picked up her napkin, and draped it across her lap.

Lee leaned closer and whispered, "Why don't you clue me in as to what's going on here."

"I don't know," she insisted.

"Yeah, right," he said sarcastically. "Where does Evans come into the picture?"

"I came with him."

"I thought you were alone."

Lee's scrutiny made her feel uncomfortable. "He got caught in the receiving line. Whoever arranged the seating must not have known we were together."

"I doubt that. You two got something going?"

Liza shushed him when Jason began to speak, welcoming them all to the celebration.

"It took Dave a long time to get around to popping the question," Jason kidded. "You'd think he would have asked her to marry him when they were seven, but he's always been slow."

"Not so slow I couldn't keep up with you," Dave called.

Laughter filled the room.

"All joking aside, the Berenson family would like to take this opportunity to welcome Dave to our family. Kit, you couldn't have done better if we'd chosen him ourselves."

He sat, and Rick stood. "The Evans family is getting the prettier addition. I can't remember a time when Kitty wasn't around, so it's only fitting that she becomes Dave's life partner. She's been his partner in every other kind of mischief you can name."

"Hey, is this a roast or an engagement party?" Kit demanded. "I might have to rethink this. Dave never mentioned his brother was a comedian." Chuckles filled the room again.

"No way," Dave said, grabbing her hand in his. "It's a tradeoff. I get your comedian, and you get mine."

Rick reached for his water glass. "Let's all toast the happy couple. May God bless their union richly, and may they provide my mother with all the grandchildren her heart desires."

This time unreserved laughter filled the room.

Jason stood again. "Pastor Clemmons, will you bless the food?"

As they ate the salads and breads that were already on the table, the waitstaff moved in and served the entrées. Liza picked up her fork and knife and cut into the chicken. It might be disguised with all sorts of other things, but she'd eaten enough of the stuff in the past year to recognize chicken when she saw it.

"You never answered my question."

She didn't have to be reminded. "Rick is a

good friend. He went off to college, then he worked overseas. Until the Evanses' party, I couldn't tell you when I saw him last. We've been renewing our friendship."

Accepting her answer, Lee immediately abandoned the conversation and launched into the subject near and dear to his heart. "Liza, we're lost without you."

"Please, Lee, not tonight. Daddy needs me," she said softly.

"He'd have a fair year without you."

"He needs a better-than-fair year, or he'll go under. There are lots of farmers being forced into bankruptcy, seeing their equipment and everything they've worked for sold at auction. No one's focusing on long-range goals. They're concentrating on survival, one year at a time."

"If he's a good farmer . . ."

"The best farmers are being forced out. I won't let that happen to Daddy. I won't," she repeated stubbornly.

"It could happen anyway, Liza."

"Not as long as there's a chance I can help prevent it. Do you have any idea how old my parents are?"

"Forty-six? Forty-seven?"

"Try fifty-six and fifty-eight."

"I thought people of their generation had children early."

"They did. My parents buried three of their children before I came along. I was born late in their lives, and I've been their life since I came along. That's the reason Daddy fights so hard to keep his farm, my birthright. I've never left home because they need me, and because I need them. I won't forsake them now, Lee."

"Nobody's asking you to do that."

"You can't farm in the dark, Lee."

"It's not fair to you."

"It's not fair to Daddy either. He's proud of the farm because he helped make it what it is. My great-great-grandfather share-cropped for years to earn the money to buy the acreage. He built the house himself. It's a legacy worth fighting for."

He clutched her hand with both of his. "I know I said I wasn't going to argue with you, but I need you."

I need you. Liza stared at Lee. How she'd longed to hear those words, only to hear them now and know he meant them in connection with the office. Not that. Never that.

He looked almost desperate. "Uncle John took off again yesterday. He's gone for a month this time. Rhonda's great with the phones, but she was out all last week with the flu. I was hoping you could get me organized again."

"A month?" she repeated. That was strange. Mr. Wilson had always been so dedicated to their clients.

"I guess he sees this as an opportunity to see if I can make the grade when the time comes for me to take over."

Liza tensed. Why did he keep bringing that up?

"Nothing will change, Liza."

"Just now when you said you needed me, did it occur to you that other people have needs, too?"

"Tell me what you need, Liza."

You, she almost shouted. No sense in being petty about it. She owed Mr. Wilson, particularly since he'd been so understanding about her extended leave of absence and continued her salary. Besides, it was her office. She'd have to contend with the mess when she returned. "Okay, Lee. You win. Sunday afternoon, after church, I'll meet you at the office."

"Thank you," he cried, grabbing her in a big bear hug. "I'm forever in your debt."

Liza managed a smile. Forever in her heart was what she preferred.

CHAPTER 9

Liza slept very little Saturday night, her mind churning with all of the things going on in her life. The need to escape was overwhelming, and after dressing, Liza left a note for her mother.

After saddling Majesty, she allowed him free rein to trot along the dirt paths. The early morning air blew the cobwebs and night's dreams away, giving Liza a fresh outlook on the day.

The breezes rustled through cornstalks, their whisper like that of a woman in silk walking. Dew glistened on the grass like newly cut diamonds. Liza spotted a large garden spider and stopped to marvel at the web he'd woven between two large old oaks. The dew made the unique pattern even more evident.

Though not many acres, the farm still required a lot of attention and expertise. Her father was born and bred to this life.

Would she be as successful?

In the Bible, James compared patience in suffering to how a farmer waited for the land to yield its valuable crops and how the farmer waited for the autumn and spring rains. She certainly was beginning to understand the concept of patience.

Time slipped away, and Liza knew she needed to make an appearance at home before her parents began to worry. After taking care of Majesty and the other chores, she washed up on the back porch.

In the kitchen, the refrigerator door opened with a gentle tug. She poured juice for everyone, then contemplated the breakfast choices. Deciding on pancakes, she pulled out a carton of eggs and the other ingredients.

"Morning, Mom," she said, chuckling as the woman's gaze flashed protectively about her kitchen. Liza gave her a quick peck on the cheek and removed milk from the refrigerator. Stirring the pancake batter, she said, "I was going to surprise you with breakfast in bed."

"It would have been a surprise," her mother agreed, bending to pick up a tiny fragment of eggshell from the floor. "Drink your juice," she said, passing Liza the glass.

Liza took a couple of sips, then set the

glass on the counter before she rummaged for a frying pan. "Where is that flat one I like so much?" She jumped back when the pile unbalanced and several pans slid onto the floor.

"Honey, as much as I appreciate your efforts . . ."

"Okay, I get the message. You hate people in your kitchen. I'll go shower for church."

Liza whistled cheerily as she went upstairs. Her father slept in the downstairs bedroom at the front of the house so she wasn't concerned about waking him, although she knew he was already wide awake.

The cool water felt wonderful as it washed away the stickiness from her early morning activity. After she toweled dry, Liza slipped into a sleeveless knit dress she liked to wear around home and went to see her father. He sat on the edge of his bed, putting on his robe.

"Hello, Pops," she said, smoothing back the hair on his forehead and kissing him there. "How are you feeling?"

"I'll get by, I guess. No real complaints, other than this thing," he said, slapping a hand against the despised cast.

"You'll have one on your hand if you keep that up," Liza warned. "It won't be much longer."

"Dr. Mayes said another three weeks. That's pretty long, if you ask me."

"It is," she consoled, patting his hand, "but you're blessed, Daddy. You're alive, and, God willing, in a few weeks, you'll be able to walk again. You still have your leg and your life."

"I know that," he allowed, "but, honey, I'm out of my element here. I need to be doing my work — not laying around, forcing you to do it."

Liza gazed sympathetically at his stricken face. He was like a child whose favorite toy had been taken away. "I wish you were out there, but I'd rather see you well again than see this farm make thousands of dollars. Your health is worth much more than that. If anything had happened to you . . ."

She dropped down on the bed and wrapped her arms about his neck. "You're right there with me every minute of the day."

"Liza, baby, you're worth a dozen sons and daughters. I love you."

"I love you, too, Daddy," she whispered.

"I know."

"Let me help you to the kitchen."

"I'm too slow. Better go eat your breakfast. It's getting on toward church time."

Back in the kitchen, Liza said, "Let me get some flowers for the table." She ran out

159

the door, smack-dab into Lee.

"Ah, the farmer's daughter," he drawled after getting a glimpse of her bare feet.

"Why, of course," she drawled, emphasizing her Southern accent. "Just a li'l ol' farmer's daughter who loves the feel of God's good country dirt under her feet. Don't y'all?" She fluttered her long eyelashes at him.

Liza started at the admiring glint in the laughter-filled eyes. "I all wouldn't know," he said. "I all's from the city. We only have good city concrete."

"Why, you poor thing," Liza said, walking around to the backyard.

Lee trailed after her. "You really think so?"

She cut both a yellow and a peach-colored rose and breathed their heady aromas. "No. It was the best life for you, I suppose. What brings you to our neck of the woods?"

"I thought I'd see if I could do anything for you this morning since you're doing me a favor this afternoon."

"You really are a city boy. I've been up since dawn." She didn't add that part of the time had been spent on horseback.

"I thought there was always something to do on a farm."

"The Sabbath is a much-needed day

of rest."

He shrugged. "You can't say I didn't offer."

There was something not right about his early morning appearance. "Come on, Lee, you know this visit is suspect, at best."

His whistle pierced the air. "I give in," he said, holding up his hands and crying, "Truce. Cease-fire. If I had a white flag, I'd wave it."

Liza's face turned red.

"I honestly did want to help. I feel guilty about heaping more on you with all your work here. How are your parents?"

That didn't sound like a selfish act. Was he beginning to understand? Liza sighed, shaking her head. "I've never known anyone like you."

"Because I asked about your parents?" Lee asked, mischief glinting in his eyes.

"You really get a kick out of keeping people guessing."

"This is a beautiful spot," Lee said, stepping closer. Their gaze met, and his lips slowly descended to meet hers. Like a moth to a flame, Liza felt herself being pulled in. She was powerless to resist his kiss.

"Liza, where are those flowers?" her mother called.

Lee's smile was as intimate as the kiss

when he bent to retrieve them from the ground.

"Here, Mom," she managed, taking them from him and hurrying toward the house. "I'd have been in a few minutes ago if a certain early visitor hadn't waylaid me in the garden."

Her mother pushed the screen door open and greeted Lee with a warm smile. "Lee! Come in. How have you been?"

"Fine, Mrs. Stephens. And you?" He eyed Liza as she attempted to retrieve a vase just out of reach. "Let me get that."

He handed it to her. "I asked after you a few minutes ago, and your daughter tried to pick a fight."

"Liza!" her mother exclaimed.

"It was his fault, Mom."

"I'd declare you were enemies if I didn't know better."

Liza glanced at Lee, wondering what he thought about her mother's statement.

"Sometimes we are," he said. "All good friends should be at times."

Mrs. Stephens set the filled plates on the table, resting her hand on her husband's shoulder as he shook pills from the containers. "Maybe so," she allowed. "Make yourself at home. Would you care for breakfast?"

"I wouldn't mind coffee."

Paul Stephens snorted.

"This is a no-coffee environment," Liza said. "There's juice or milk in the refrigerator. The glasses are over there," she added, pointing to a pristine white cabinet.

Lee laughed heartily, his deep laughter sounding throughout the kitchen. "Don't put yourself out on my account."

"I won't," she said, continuing to pour syrup over her pancakes.

"Sarah Elizabeth Stephens," her mother wailed, returning the tray to the countertop. "Have you forgotten your manners?"

Liza leaned her elbow on the table and rested her chin in her hand. "Most of them."

"What did I ever do to deserve this?" her mother entreated, lifting her gaze heavenward.

"Okay, Mom," she relented, passing Lee the plate of untouched pancakes. "Excuse me, please. I have to dress for church. Mom, Lee says thanks for breakfast."

"That child," her mother said, shaking her head as Liza left the room. "You'll have to excuse her. We spoiled her terribly."

"She really is delightful," Lee said.

Liza heard them talking as she walked toward the stairs. She didn't need her mother sharing all of her secrets with Lee. The sooner she returned, the better.

Liza dashed for the stairs. She came down minutes later dressed in a pale green, two-piece summer suit, her long hair flowing down her back, the bangs secured in a barrette.

Lee stood and watched her cross the room. "Would you like an escort to church?"

"You want to go to church with me?"

He shrugged. "Sure. If you think I'm dressed okay."

Far removed from the suits she generally saw him in, Liza found Lee quite handsome in his casual khaki slacks and short-sleeved, button-down shirt.

"Of course, I'm not Rick Evans."

"No, you aren't," Liza agreed.

"Your lifelong friend. Will we ever be friends like that?"

Liza picked up her purse and Bible.

There was a great deal of difference between liking a man as a friend and being in love with him. Awareness generated a chemistry of its own. "We are friends, Lee."

"If you say so. Sometimes I think you really do dislike me."

"We'll be late for church," she reminded, taking a step toward the door.

"Then let's go, but don't think this is the last of it." His expression grew more determined as he held the screen door open. "I'm going to be your friend yet."

CHAPTER 10

Liza settled comfortably into his car, watching the familiar scenery roll by. "I can't believe half of July is already gone. Doesn't seem possible that we'll get it all done, but Daddy declares we will, and he's the expert."

Lee glanced at her, then brought his gaze back to the road. "What I know about farming, you could put on the sharp end of a stickpin."

"That much, huh?" Liza grinned.

"City through and through," he agreed.

"Well, you're a country lawyer now, and you're going to have to learn better."

"Yes, ma'am," he agreed solemnly. "What does a greenhorn like me do to 'learn better'?"

Liza hesitated, blinking as the crazy thought coursed through her head. What if he spent a day with her on her own ground? No way. "Come for dinner one night. You can pick Daddy's brain."

"Sounds like a plan to me," he said, parking the car in the church lot and coming around to open her door. "Of course, with all the experience you're getting, I'll have my own resident expert in the office."

Attending church with Lee resulted in curious reactions from the people she'd known all her life. Several members came forward to ask after her parents and who her gentleman friend was. Every time, Lee stuck out his hand and introduced himself before Liza could explain. Most people said how glad they were to have him there and invited him to come back soon. She almost felt his sigh of relief when they sat down in the pew.

"Nice church."

Liza agreed. The congregation had bought the land and built the new sanctuary only two years before. The stained glass windows depicted a number of biblical scenes and sparkled beautifully in the sunlight. The padded pews were much more comfortable than the old wooden ones.

"How long have you attended?"

"Since before I was born. My ancestors were charter members. Mom and Dad married here."

"That's quite a history."

The minister of music stepped forward and directed them to secure a hymnal and turn to page one. Lee stopped Liza when she reached for a second book. "We can share."

The opening music of "Holy, Holy, Holy" filled the sanctuary, and the words of praise to her Lord poured from Liza. She noted the way Lee looked at her, almost as if shocked.

As was normal practice, the pastor welcomed the members of the congregation and asked them to turn and greet their neighbors. More people came forth to welcome Lee.

"Friendly bunch," he whispered when the music began again. "By the way, you have a beautiful voice."

Liza smiled. "Thank you."

Pastor Clemmons stepped into the pulpit minutes later. "Today I want to speak to you on your witness for Christ. For those who would like to read with me, turn in your Bible to Romans 12:1."

Liza quickly flipped through the tissue-thin pages to the chapter and verse he named and leaned to share with Lee.

" 'Therefore, I urge you, brothers, in view of God's mercy, to offer your bodies as living sacrifices, holy and pleasing to God —

this is your spiritual act of worship,' " he read.

"What kind of witness are you? When people look at you, do they see Jesus in your actions?"

Thinking of the picture she'd presented to Lee with her combative behavior, Liza squirmed inwardly. How could she ever hope to show him God's love when she constantly battled him?

True, she prayed for him daily. Though she knew a wise Christian woman would never consider a relationship with a man who didn't share her beliefs, she allowed herself to ask "what if" more than she really should. If he couldn't understand why she had to help her parents, how could she ever think he would willingly accept her beliefs?

Perhaps she was being judgmental. The sermon continued as the thoughts coursed through her head. The pastor definitely caught her attention with his next words.

"Examine your actions daily. Ask yourself: Would Jesus have behaved this way? Remember that people have certain expectations of believers. Sadly, more often than not, they're looking for that one little slip, be it anger or a weakening of spirit, to say, 'I knew you weren't what you claim to be.'

"What they fail to realize is that we're all

sinners — sinners saved by the grace of our heavenly Father. People with all the human failings who have been made whole by the love of the Lord. As we sing the closing hymn, the altar is open to all. If you haven't experienced God's grace for yourself, step out into the aisle and take those first difficult steps."

Two of the youth stepped out into the aisle, and Liza's heart filled with joy. Each time someone made the decision, she was moved to tears. She glanced at Lee. He seemed lost in thought.

They continued to sing as the pastor prayed with the new converts. He introduced them to the congregation and asked everyone to extend the right hand of fellowship to their new brothers in Christ.

Liza felt torn — she knew these boys and wanted to speak to them, yet she hated to delay Lee for fear he would be uncomfortable.

"Go ahead. I'll wait here."

She smiled and stepped into the line forming down the aisle. Several times, she glanced back to see church members stopping to speak to Lee.

Within minutes she was back, gathering her Bible and purse. "Ready whenever you are."

"I told your mom I was treating you to lunch. Anything special?"

"Why don't we pick up something and take it back to the office?"

"The least I can do is take you to a decent restaurant."

In reality, she would love to have him take her to a nice restaurant, but it wasn't meant to be. There were differences in their lives that allowed friendship but certainly precluded a relationship — the first being Lee's lack of awareness of her feelings for him.

"I really don't have much time. If we eat while we work, we can get lots more done."

"Okay," he agreed, sounding reluctant. "But promise you'll let me make it up to you."

They discussed the fast-food possibilities and ran through the drive-in of a local chicken place Liza liked. After they bought their food and drinks, Lee drove to the office.

Well, Lord, a few seconds to organize my thoughts would have been nice, Liza thought, but an opportunity immediately presented itself to make things right between Lee and herself. "Today's sermon really danced on my toes. I apologize for being so prickly lately. I haven't given you much reason to believe I'm a follower of Christ."

"You're kidding, right?"

Confusion filled her. "No."

"Liza, I marvel at your goodness and kindness. Sure, you get angry. Everyone does when they're shoved against the wall. I'm the one who owes you an apology. I've pushed you ever since I came to the office, never stopping to think about all you do there. I came from a partnership with a huge list of names on the door. I knew there was no hope I'd ever see my name there. We had lawyers, paralegals, secretaries, and investigators so eager to advance, they stabbed each other in the back to accomplish their personal goals. I'm career oriented, but not like that.

"I realized today that this job isn't your life. It's only part of who you are. Your religion, your family, your friends, and lots of other things fit into that picture as well. I know I'm spoiled. All my life, my parents catered to my every whim. Since I was the only grandchild in the family, Uncle John and Uncle Dennis did their share to help. 'Me' has been the biggest word in my dictionary for a long time. In the past, everything centered on what I wanted, when and how. Thanks to you, I'm beginning to think it shouldn't be that way."

Lee parked the car and took the bag with

their lunch. Flabbergasted, Liza grabbed the soda cups and followed him inside. Stepping into the office was like coming home, and she smiled to herself upon realizing nothing had changed.

She missed her work and felt a sudden longing to return. The situation presented an entirely different dilemma for her. Her parents weren't always going to be around, and one day she would be forced to choose between her job and the farm.

In her heart, Liza knew the office would win out, but she didn't want to disappoint her parents either. No sense borrowing trouble. She had plenty on her plate right now.

"Let's take this into the break room."

"But, Lee, we don't have much time."

"We can take time to eat our lunch," he said, overriding her protest with an easy smile. "Besides, I'd prefer not to have your greasy prints all over my papers."

They spread the meal on the table and sat down. Liza whispered grace and started to eat.

"I enjoyed your church this morning."

"I'm glad. You know Mr. Wilson attends First Church on Madison Street, don't you?"

"I've seen that church."

"Why don't you attend church regularly, Lee?"

"Believe it or not, my parents took me to church every week. I believe in God and His grace and majesty, but I've let other stuff become more important over the years. I also happen to believe there's a certain commitment to religion."

"You mean a focus like you have on law?"

"Well, yes. I know it's important to attend and participate in church, but I have so much going on in my life that I just don't have time."

"Jesus took time to die for your sins," Liza reminded. "Sorry. There's that witness thing again. Guess I came on too strong."

"Sometimes it takes strong to make people understand. And you're right. I shouldn't wait until it's convenient for me. I'll think about what you've said."

"That's all anyone can ask." Liza tore open a wet wipe and cleaned her hands. "We'd better get to work."

"You can't be finished already?"

She glanced at the remainder of her meal and felt guilty at her wastefulness. "My eyes were bigger than my stomach."

Lee started packing his food in the box.

"No. Finish eating. I know where to start."

He leaned back and asked, "Is that how

you lost the weight?"

Liza could hardly tell him being in his presence curbed her appetite. "I ate enough." She left him in the kitchen, finishing his meal.

The place was a mess. The in-basket overflowed into the out-basket with files, transcription tapes, and mail.

"You're kidding, right?" she asked minutes later when he walked in. "This would take a lifetime to clear up."

"We're not exactly the most organized lawyers when it comes to the office. Tell me what to do."

Every time he made a statement like that, the craziest thoughts ran through her head. What would he think if she told him what she really wanted from him?

He glanced at her curiously. "Liza?"

She leaned against the desk. "Why don't you sort through that jumble?" She indicated the pile on the right side of the desk. "Put the files and tapes in stacks, then separate your mail from Mr. Wilson's. After you finish sorting, check the files and put away those you've finished with. I'll see if I can determine what Rhonda has typed."

He grabbed a chair and sat down in front of the desk. "Thanks, Liza."

She nodded, recalling the number of times

he'd accused her of being disloyal to the office. *Stop it,* she chided. *Remember you're supposed to be a good witness.*

Liza found only a couple of tapes hadn't been completed and slipped the first cassette into the transcription machine. Only a small amount of actual typing needed to be completed — a few letters, a will, and a couple of briefs.

There was a point of inquiry on one of the briefs, and Liza went to the research library for the volume she needed. She spotted it on the top shelf and pulled the ladder over.

When the book didn't move, she pulled harder, the tug dislodging the book along with three others stacked carelessly on top. Liza overbalanced and fell back on the carpeted floor. The heavy volumes thudded about her.

"Liza? What happened?"

The room went dark as the last volume smacked her on top of the head.

She awoke to find Lee leaning over her prone form. "That hurt," she moaned, her hand automatically going to her forehead.

"I've told Rhonda at least half a dozen times to put them back where they belong. She has this thing for stacking and putting them away later. I should have warned you."

Liza struggled to sit up, feeling woozy from her encounter with the thick text. "She'll kill somebody."

"Are you okay?" Lee asked, his fingers gentle as he touched the bump on her forehead.

She nodded. "I'll have a whopper of a headache tomorrow, though."

Lee helped her up off the floor and to the waiting room sofa where he placed a pillow beneath her head and demanded she lie still. "I'll be right back."

He returned with an improvised ice bag, which he rested against her forehead. Liza winced at the coldness of the cloth, gradually accepting the numbing effect. She moved to sit up, holding it in place. "Thanks. This is helping."

"Lie still," Lee commanded, resting his arm across the chair as he sat on the edge. "I'll take you to the hospital."

She savored the satisfaction of his concern but felt an overpowering need to reassure him. "No, I'll be okay. Honestly. We Stephenses have tough heads."

"We should file a worker's comp form," he said, pushing her shoulder back to the sofa.

So much for caring. "Let me up, Lee," she insisted.

"No more work."

"What's the matter? Afraid I'll sue you?"

He managed a weak grin. "Very funny."

"For heaven's sake," she cried when he trailed after her into the library. "You're worse than a mother hen with one biddy. Give me that volume," she requested. "No, the other one."

Liza took the reference book back to her desk. She accepted the aspirin and water Lee brought, thanking him briefly before dropping her gaze back to the book.

She couldn't help but be aware of the way he watched her, almost hovering over her desk as he sorted and filed. He had gone through to Mr. Wilson's office to put some papers on his desk when she finished the brief and called out to him, "Lee, I've got . . ."

His look was anxious when he rushed out, relief obvious when he realized she was okay. "Does your head still hurt?"

"Not really. It's more like a dull throb. I need to get home to feed the animals."

"I called the hospital. They said I should bring you in."

She rolled her eyes. "They would. Believe me, it's not that bad. Take me home. I'll be fine tomorrow."

"I heard that you're not supposed to sleep

after a head injury."

"It's at least five hours before bedtime."

She preceded Lee out the door, waiting for him to lock up. He took her arm, ignoring her protests that she could walk by herself. Lee unlocked the door, handing her into the vehicle with great care. He pushed away her fumbling hands and fastened her safety belt. Her heart pounded at his closeness, and Liza was glad when he backed away from her.

She leaned back in the seat, the smooth hum of the motor making her drowsy.

"Liza, wake up." Lee shook her arm, then depressed the window control to fill the car with cool evening air. "Are you all right?"

"I wasn't asleep. Just resting my eyes."

"You always breathe that deeply when you're resting your eyes? We can turn on the radio or talk," he said, offering two practical solutions. "Just don't go to sleep."

"All right," she muttered, shifting forward in the seat to fiddle with the knobs. She watched him out of the corner of her eye, seeing his curious expression.

"You can't find anything to say to me, can you, Liza?"

She frowned at his accurate evaluation of the situation. The entire day had been a big mistake. It only served to increase her agony over loving someone she could never have as more than a friend. She had to be strong. She couldn't let him know her true feelings.

"We can exchange all the pleasantries you like."

"What happened, Liza?"

"I don't know what you mean." She tuned the dial to a Christian station. She adjusted the volume, almost drowning out his voice.

Lee frowned and reached to lower the volume. "Yes, you do. We used to be friends. What happened?"

"Why do you keep asking that? We're friends. We don't see each other as often, nor do we have the same things in common. Like most people, it's awkward when we meet."

"You see to that," he agreed. The car surged forward as he depressed the accelerator. "I wouldn't want to keep you in my company a moment longer than necessary."

When he stopped at the house, Liza fumbled with the door handle in her haste to get out of the car. "By the way, tell Rhonda to put those books away before she really hurts someone. And tell her to check those . . . Lee!" she protested when his hand went to the back of her neck and pulled her forward, his lips touching hers. She wrenched away, hiding the vulnerability in her eyes. "Can't you behave?"

"Who'd want me to?" he inquired. "Certainly not you."

"It'd be a nice change. To finish what I was saying, tell Rhonda to check the tapes for some research Mr. Wilson wants done. Good-bye."

Liza got out of the car and moved toward the house, intent on changing clothes and feeding up, only to find Lee right behind her. "Where do you think you're going?" she demanded.

"To help with the chores."

"Not in those clothes."

"I'm not leaving."

"Oh, all right," Liza conceded ungraciously. "Come in."

Her mother was watching television in the family room when Liza showed Lee into the room. "He insists on helping me, even though I told him he's not dressed properly."

"It's the least I can do." Lee launched into the story of Liza's injury, raising her mother's concern.

She frowned at both of them. "I'm going to change."

"Are you sure you're okay?" her mother asked.

Liza nodded and hurried upstairs.

"Why don't you visit with Mom?" she suggested a few minutes later.

"Stop trying to discourage me. I said I'd help, and I intend to."

She scowled at him. "Stubborn."

"Right back at you."

In the barn, Liza found the feed bin was empty and went into the storeroom. Refusing to ask for help, she hefted the fifty-pound bag into the wheelbarrow. She caught her hand underneath. "Ouch!"

"Are you trying to kill yourself?" Lee lifted the bag. He reached for her hand, holding it between his own as he checked for damage.

"No," she denied. "Let go. I can take care of it."

"No, you can't. You think you're the most self-sufficient person in the world. Sometimes you even manage to act like it, but I know differently. You're as needy as the next person, and it's time you realized the truth."

She glared at him. "You don't know me very well at all, Lee. I have the support of people I love. I don't need another mother or father. You're the one who needs people when the mood strikes — when you're ready to take advantage to fulfill your own agenda."

Liza's voice rose until she was yelling at him. The pain in her head and hand didn't compare to the ache in her heart. She hated this bickering caused by her overwhelming awareness of him. It was driving her crazy. "Go home, Lee," she cried brokenly, her eyes glistening with unshed tears.

He took a step back. "I'm sorry. I can't."

"Please." The tears were flowing freely down her face. "Just go."

He stepped toward her. "Liza —"

"No, Lee." She pushed him away. "Just go. Please."

"I'm sorry, but I can't leave you like this. You have to calm down." He pulled her into his arms.

"I am calm," she whispered against his chest, her voice breaking as she allowed herself to remain in his arms. Realizing what was happening, she pulled away. "Please leave."

"I'll go, Liza, but remember — you're the one who keeps pushing me out of your life."

Lee walked from the barn without so much as a backward glance. All the strength drained from her legs, and she dropped onto a nearby bale of hay, her head resting in her hands as she gave way to the threatening sobs. She heard him return, and her gaze was drawn upward, meeting his.

"Liza?" he whispered, his face ghastly white in the late-afternoon light.

"Just stop, Lee," she moaned, turning away from him. "Stop saying things like that. You play on my vulnerability, begging me time and time again to be someone I'm not. Don't ask me to give any more. I can't handle it. Go away. I don't want you here."

This time he didn't return. Liza sat in the barn for some time, considering what she should do. Her prolonged absence brought her mother in search of her. "I heard Lee leave. I thought you finished."

"Sorry. I lost track of the time."

"What's going on with you two? I could hear you yelling out here, clear in the house."

Oh, Mom, if you only knew. Lee was gone, this time without so much as a good-bye . . . and she'd driven him away. "He doesn't understand."

"Neither do I. I know you're attracted to him."

"He's not a Christian, Mom."

"I see."

Liza wished she did. She didn't see anything but heartache for allowing herself to fall for a man she couldn't have.

"He went to church with you today."

"And look how it ended."

"Never doubt the power of God," her mother said. "Remember He's capable of changing all things we can't understand. Everything will be all right, if you trust Him."

"How, Mom?"

"Where's your faith, Liza? I know you believe in miracles. Don't you think God can work a miracle for you and Lee?"

"It would take one."

"It's getting late. You need to finish up and come inside."

Later, much later, after she finally went to bed, Liza gave way to the tears. They flowed until she could cry no longer. She lay wide awake for the next several hours, her mind refusing to forget what had happened that day.

CHAPTER 11

Lee's words continued to play around in Liza's head. Did she push him out? Yes, but only because he wanted more than she could offer right now.

With days that started at the crack of dawn and ended late at night, Liza felt bone tired. Tonight was the first night in weeks she promised herself a break, and she left the supper table without offering to help with the cleanup. In the family room, she stretched out on the sofa and settled in to watch a little television. Maybe later she'd call Kitty to see how the wedding plans were progressing.

Lately she'd worked twice as hard to accomplish the tasks she wanted finished. As if their farm didn't demand enough, she volunteered to help the neighbors in whatever capacity she could. Of course, she felt she owed favors to everyone; but at the rate she was paying them back, it might not take the rest of her life.

There hadn't been much time for a social life lately. Not that it mattered. She didn't feel like seeing other people. By the time she finished work each evening, the thought of going out lacked appeal, and she often ended up eating dinner with her parents and going to bed early.

The phone rang, and she pushed herself up to reach for it. "Liza," Kitty called cheerily. "Just the person I wanted to talk to."

"What's up?"

"Your friends are feeling like you don't have time for us anymore."

"I've been busy."

"I know, but Dave and I were talking. What if we come over and bring a movie, or just play games?"

So much for her quiet evening. "Sure. Come on over. Look for me in the family room. I'm the lump on the sofa."

Kit giggled. "Girl, you've got to get some exercise."

"Please don't mention that word in my presence."

Liza hung up the phone and went upstairs to exchange her old shorts and shirt for a sleeveless blouse and Capri pants. She was making popcorn when Kitty let herself in.

"We're here," Kitty announced, hugging

Liza. Dave and Rick followed on her heels.

"Just in time to help with the snacks," Liza said, hugging each one. "What does everyone want to drink?"

They agreed on soda, and everyone pitched in. Carrying their food into the sitting room, they chatted through the movie credits.

"I figured you'd rather watch a movie than do anything to work your brain," Dave said.

"My brain thanks you." She glanced at Rick's glass. "You need a refill."

"I wouldn't if you two hadn't added a box of salt to the popcorn. My mouth is as dry as the Sahara."

"You were the one who bumped my shoulder," Liza said, throwing a kernel in his direction.

He retaliated, and Liza caught it in her mouth, grinning at his surprised look. "You coming over tomorrow?"

"For what?"

Liza slipped her hands beneath her hair, lifting it up and over the back of the sofa. "To be in the way."

"That's the truth of it," Rick admitted. "Your dad was bragging on you yesterday. Said you're doing beautifully."

She shook her head in denial. "I couldn't have done it alone."

Dave let go of Kitty's hand and leaned forward. "Don't be so modest. You're doing a wonderful job. We couldn't do better ourselves, could we, Rick?"

"You're making it look easy," Rick agreed. "Want to share your secret?"

Slightly embarrassed by their tag-team compliments, Liza made a joke out of the situation. "No way. I might need a job next year. Your dad can hire me on. Of course, he'd have to hire my team of experts — most of the town, in fact. Everyone's been so helpful."

"It's a community, Liza," Kitty said. "Friends help friends. You've done your bit as well. How many times a week do you go out of your way to help someone else?"

"As often as possible, but everyone's been so good to us. We'll never be able to pay them back."

"They don't expect you to," Rick told her.

Liza knew they didn't. The eggs she'd eaten for breakfast came from a nearby farm. For lunch, they'd eaten cake a neighbor brought over. One man visited with her dad while his wife took advantage of the opportunity to get her mom out of the house. Even the children brought handfuls of wildflowers they hoped would brighten Mr. Paul's day.

She knew farmers shared a belief in hard work, commitment to family, community, and rural life. It was certainly obvious as the neighborhood helped them through each and every day.

Liza sat on the sofa beside Rick, twisting until she got comfortable. Tomorrow she needed to pick butter beans. Her mother hadn't had time to do it, not with taking care of her father and the house and helping around the farm.

She thought she had it rough, but Liza had recognized her dad's cabin fever from the beginning. He was starting to help outside more and grew so irritable at times that he shouted at her. Her mother just shook her head and gave her one of those "don't argue" looks.

Not that he complained all of the time. She couldn't forget the look on his face when one visitor told him what a fine job she was doing. "More dedicated than my boy, that's for sure. I should have had a girl."

"That's right," her father agreed, catching her hand and giving it a gentle squeeze. "Wouldn't take anything for her."

"Maybe we can marry her off to my boy," their neighbor suggested, winking at Liza.

She felt her cheeks burn at their teasing.

"I'm going inside before you start talking dowry."

The men laughed, their conversation turning to a recent fishing trip.

Kit asked her a question, and Liza pulled her attention to the movie. After seeing the trailers on television, she had planned to see the movie in the theater but never made it.

The movie ended, and they turned to the nightly news.

"I don't like the look of this one," Dave said when the weatherman talked about Hurricane Bobby.

"You think it'll make landfall?" Liza asked. Her dad had mentioned the storm's projected path that morning, but she hadn't thought about it much. Most days, she just hoped it wouldn't rain until after dark.

"This area hasn't been too blessed in the past few years. They're coming in near Wilmington."

"Losing electricity is the worst part," Kit said. "Mom almost lost the contents of her freezer with that storm last year. She made sure Daddy bought a generator after that. Said she put too many hours into freezing those vegetables to lose them."

"And you lost those long, hot baths and showers you're so fond of," Liza teased.

Kit grimaced at her. "We didn't have water for three days."

"You're supposed to make preparations," Liza reminded. "Things like filling the bathtub so you have water."

"I hate bird baths," Kitty said, looking at Dave. "You know, if we lived in town we'd always have water and sewer services."

"And I'd have a commute every time I needed to do something at the farm. Sorry, honey, you're marrying a farm boy. There's always the pond if you're desperate."

Kitty made a face and pretended to shiver. "No thanks."

"Like you've never swam there before," Dave mocked.

"Let's pray this one goes out to sea and does no harm," Liza said.

"Amen," Rick agreed.

"Fill me in on the wedding plans."

"We're about ready to elope," Dave said. "We've come to the conclusion it takes so long to plan a wedding because you're trying to decide who to invite."

"Our mothers keep adding to the list," Kit added. "Our intimate wedding has turned into a packed house. They've decided that everyone who can't attend the ceremony should be at the reception."

"Everyone you invite won't show up," Liza

pointed out.

"We'd need the stadium if they did," Kit moaned. "Dave's not kidding. We've discussed eloping. I've got my dress, and with you and Rick to stand up for us, we could get it over with in a few hours."

Horrified they would even consider running away to get married, Liza exclaimed, "Don't do that. You'll regret not having the wedding you've always wanted."

Kitty glanced at Dave and nodded reluctantly. "I guess you're right."

Dave linked his fingers with Kit's. "I'll be glad when it's over. I can't wait to have you as my wife."

"Well, you certainly took your time asking."

"Give a man a break," he said. "I just wanted to be sure we were both ready."

Kit grinned and kissed his cheek. "Honey, I've been ready since I was ten years old."

"Back then, all you and Liza wanted to do was play bride."

Both women smiled as he triggered their memory of the times they had dressed in old castoffs and forced the guys to play their grooms.

"I won't be playing in a couple of months," Kit reminded.

Their eyes glowed with their love. They

were perfect for each other. Of course, Liza knew their friendship would change once Kit and Dave married . . . just as it had when Jason got married and dropped their foursome in favor of Judy.

For a moment, she wished it were her, then pushed the thought out of her head. Such fantasies always led to thoughts of one person. She didn't want to go there tonight.

"Guess we'd better get out of here and let you catch a couple of hours' shut-eye. Talk to you tomorrow," Kit said. "We've got to get you fitted for your dress. No poufed sleeves or flounces," she promised.

"Or big bows either, I hope?"

She hugged Liza and promised, "Sophisticated and elegant are the keywords. Well, except for the color. How do you feel about lime green or Day-Glo orange?"

Liza scowled in mock horror. "You know, I really do need to recheck my calendar. Now that I think about it, I believe I have a prior commitment."

Laughing, they headed for the door.

Liza straightened the living room and took their glasses and bowls into the kitchen. She yawned widely as she checked to make sure they were gone before turning off the outside lights and locking up for the night.

Thank You, God, for my wonderful friends.

She felt blessed to have them in her life. No matter what the future held, she would always have the love of her family and friends.

CHAPTER 12

"What else did you expect?" Liza mumbled a couple of days later when the weatherman announced coastal North Carolina was under a hurricane warning.

"Wind and rain are the farmer's worst enemies," her dad said as they sat at the breakfast table, discussing this latest problem. "Once they flatten and drown the crops, there's not much hope left."

"What do I need to do?"

"Main thing is securing everything. The yard furniture needs to go into the barn. You can turn the rockers over and tie them to porch railings. The hanging baskets and planters need to come down, too."

As the list of chores grew, Liza wondered if she'd ever get it all done. "Barney hates storms," Liza pointed out.

"Majesty, too. Hopefully we'll be on the fringes of Bobby."

Her mother slid a cooked egg onto Liza's plate.

Liza quickly placed it between two slices of toast and wrapped a paper napkin about the sandwich. "Time to get busy," she said, heading for the door. "Are we taping the windows?"

"It's not worth the trouble. The sheet of plywood for the picture window is in the barn. I don't know how you'll get it in place, though."

Liza patted her father's shoulder reassuringly. "Someone will check on us."

He reached for her hand. "Just a little more breeze and rain than normal."

As she stepped outside to begin work, Liza noticed little indication of menacing weather. The hot overcast July day felt no different from any other, but after surviving three hurricanes in two years, she knew what to expect.

The office crossed her mind. She'd heard Mr. and Mrs. Wilson were on a cruise. That left Lee on his own, with no one to tell him what to do. Later, when time allowed, she'd check with him.

A couple of hours passed, and Liza paused to mop her forehead when Lee's car pulled into the yard. "What are you doing here?" she asked when he stepped out of the car.

"Hello to you, too. I've been sent as a reinforcement. The rest of the troops couldn't make it. Kitty called and said Dave and Rick are working like crazy at their place, and she was afraid they wouldn't finish up in time to get over here."

Kitty. She should have known. That woman was a determined matchmaker. Each time they discussed the situation, her friend insisted Liza could make a difference in Lee's life.

"What about the office? Mr. Wilson's house?"

"The office is secured. I sent Rhonda home to take care of her place and went by Uncle John's before I came over here. His handyman has handled everything. He's not taking any chances."

"Daddy doesn't think we'll see much more than wind and rain, but we're not taking any chances either. I've been lugging this junk around all morning."

"Junk?"

"Well, it definitely seems that way when it's an inconvenience. I got smart and hooked up the trailer to load the lawn furniture and other small pieces. It's backed into the barn. Now all I have to do is pull it back over here and unload."

"I knew you were a smart lady. What can

I do to help?"

Liza's thoughts went to the sheet of plywood propped against the house. "I need to cover the front window."

"Let's do it."

Working together, they soon had everything finished.

"I appreciate this, Lee."

"Hey, I owe you one for helping out at the office the other day. Besides, I have been known to lend a neighborly hand now and then."

"Have you thought about where you'll go?"

"Not really. I suppose I could stay in my apartment or go to a shelter."

"Or you could stay here." When he looked surprised, she offered, "There's a spare room, if you can sleep. This storm looks like it's going to come in at night, so I doubt anyone else will."

"My adrenaline is pumping like crazy at the thought of Bobby making landfall. I suspect the excitement of my first hurricane will be enough to keep me awake as well."

"How did you know what to do?"

"Uncle John gave me a crash course before he left."

"What about Mr. and Mrs. Wilson? They aren't cruising in the middle of the storm, are they?"

"Last I heard, they're headed for Alaska."

The news pleased Liza. She didn't want to think they were in danger on open seas.

"Well, we'll just have to pray this one isn't bad." As if a portent of what was to come, the rain began to fall.

"This rain has me worried," her dad said when the downpour increased in intensity.

The forecasters kept talking about the far-reaching rain bands radiating from the distant storm and predicted an early morning landfall. Meanwhile, Liza felt a bit more apprehensive with every deluge. She dropped the curtain back into place. Darkness made it impossible to see anything.

"They're giving the new coordinates," Lee called.

Liza joined him on the sofa. The stations had been running continuous coverage ever since the warning went into effect, making announcements, and keeping everyone current on Hurricane Bobby's coordinates. The weatherman repeated the warning, indicating the storm's extent on the map.

"Looks like he's veering this way," Lee said. "How much rain is too much?" he asked her father after watching Liza plot the coordinates on a hurricane map she kept nearby.

"It's hard to say. If the rain keeps up like this until daylight, I'm sure we'll have some serious flooding."

"Now, Paul, what does the Bible tell you about worrying? You're not helping yourself at all."

"I know, Sarah, but —"

"No buts," she insisted, reaching for his hand. "Let's pray about this and leave it to the Lord."

When her mother began to pray, Liza glanced at Lee to find he had bowed his head. After her mother spoke her words to Jesus, her father took over and prayed for His mercy to surround them during this storm and keep them safe. Liza added a hearty *amen* and smiled when Lee did the same.

Around ten thirty, her mother insisted on getting a snack and something to drink. Liza went into the kitchen to help. Back in the family room, all four of them were watching the news updates when the phone rang.

It was Kitty, and she was in a mood to chat. "Yes, Lee helped out. He's here now, waiting out the storm with us." Liza could hardly answer her friend's questions with Lee sitting at her side. She hoped he hadn't heard Kit's excited gasp. "This rain is incredible," she said instead. "I hate waiting around to see what's going to happen."

She almost laughed when Kitty said, "Girl, you've got a handsome man sitting there with you, and you're worried about time. You better seize the moment."

"Any progress on the plans?" Liza asked, ignoring her friend's advice.

"We're getting there. This dream wedding I always thought I wanted isn't what it's cut out to be. In fact, it's a lot of hard work. Right now, I'd like nothing better than to go down after church, say our vows, and take off on our honeymoon."

"So has Dave filled you in on the dream honeymoon?"

"No," she pouted. "It'll be a miracle if I can get him away from the farm for that long. He'll probably want to go to some farming convention."

"I don't think so. Dave's going to make a wonderful husband."

"I know. I just hate competing with the farm."

"Don't think of it as a competition. It's his career choice. You'd better get used to it now, or you'll be miserable."

"I know. I really do love Dave, and I know he's the man God intends for me. He's been farming for most of the time we've dated, so I have a pretty good idea what our life will be like."

"I don't mean it in a bad way, Kit. But when people are happy in their chosen career fields, that's one less problem a couple has to contend with."

"Amen to that. Wow, listen to that wind. I'd better go. Mom's got the guest list out, and she's waiting for me to hang up. I told her it's late, but she says we won't sleep anyway. Would you please tell me why it's an insult not to invite cousins I haven't seen in ten years to my wedding?"

"It is a good time to get your family together."

"Yeah, but I hate it when people I haven't heard from in a long time suddenly remember I exist."

"Particularly when a gift is involved," Liza added.

"Exactly."

A sudden loud crash caught Liza's attention.

"What was that?" Kit demanded.

The same words echoed about the room. Lee and her mother jumped from their seats. Her dad followed at a slower pace. "Gotta run, Kit. Something just happened outside."

"Be careful."

The others were looking out the kitchen

window. "See anything?" Liza asked, straining to see for herself.

"No. It's pitch-black dark out there. I think something fell on the house," her father said.

"I could probably see better from the upstairs windows," Liza suggested.

"It might not be safe," her mother said quickly.

"I'll go with her," Lee said.

Liza was glad to let Lee lead the way as they moved from room to room.

"Found it." Lee pulled back the curtain at her bedroom window to reveal the large pine tree resting against the house.

"Can you tell if the roof's leaking?" Liza asked, studying the ceiling. There were no signs of water damage.

"Doesn't appear to be. Let's get a flashlight, and I'll go outside and see how bad it is."

Following him down the stairs, Liza protested, "You can't go out in this."

"Just long enough to take a look. Put up a tarp if it's needed."

"Let me get the raincoats. I'll go with you."

"Stay inside. No sense in both of us getting wet."

In the hall closet, Liza pulled yellow slickers off hangers. "Then you should stay in. You're the guest."

Her parents stepped into the hallway. "What happened?"

"That pine on my side of the house snapped. It's resting on the roof. We're going to check it out."

"Give me my coat."

"No, Daddy."

"We'll take care of it, sir," Lee said.

Her mother jumped into the fray. "You're not going out there, Paul. I don't care if the tree comes into the house. You're not strong enough to fight that wind and rain."

"I am not a weakling, Sarah."

Liza slipped on her boots. "Listen to Mom, Daddy. I'll check and come right back in."

Lee snapped the hooks on the raincoat he wore. "And I'm going with her."

The force of the winds nearly took her breath away as Liza opened the kitchen door. The moment she moved from the steps, Liza realized just how much rain had fallen. The yard was flooded, water coming up around her ankles.

Ducking his head, Lee grabbed her hand and pulled her around the side of the house, flashing the powerful beam of the light toward the roofline. The tree appeared to have broken the face board around the top and knocked in the roof a bit, but as far as she could tell, it hadn't gone through.

"Do we need to cover it?" Liza shouted.

Lee shook his head.

They splashed back around the house, avoiding fallen limbs. Inside the kitchen, they removed their shoes and dumped them into the box her mom kept for that purpose. Sarah handed them towels while her father impatiently demanded a report.

"There's some damage. We'll be able to tell more in the morning. The yard's flooded." Liza pointed to the watermark on Lee's pants leg.

Her mother quickly crossed the room to her father's side. "It'll be fine, Paul. We'll get through this."

Paul Stephens wrapped his arms about his wife, holding her tight. After so many years, they were even more in love. They looked to each other for support during bad times. Liza constantly prayed to one day find love as strong as theirs.

"Is he okay?" Lee asked softly.

"I should have kept my mouth shut about the flooding. He's already worried about the crops."

"You can't keep it a secret. He's not blind."

"True. Thanks for going out there with me. It's nasty."

"Weather's not even fit for ducks. Let's go see if we can cheer them up."

While they were out, her mother had set the lanterns and candles about the room. A battery-operated radio sat on the coffee table.

"It's just a matter of time before we lose power," she explained, handing Lee a pair of socks. "I can't offer you pants, but I figured you would appreciate these."

Lee cuffed his khakis several times and pulled on the dry socks. "Thanks, Mrs. Stephens."

True to her prediction, they lost power within the hour. Liza flipped on the radio, and they listened to the deejays talk nonstop about the storm that had given everyone a common cause. No music punctuated their discussion as they allowed callers to describe their storm experiences. The announcers issued constant warnings to stay inside. They talked about the eye of the hurricane, warning the population not to assume the storm was over when the calm arrived.

Their small group sat in silence, hearing the fury of the wind and rain as it battered the house. Now and again, one of them commented about an act of stupidity the announcer reported on the radio.

"Back when I was a young man, Hazel ripped through the area," her dad said. "That lady did a lot of damage. Almost wiped out some areas."

"Back in the old days, they named all the hurricanes after women. At least they're equal-opportunity storms now," Liza joked.

Lee jostled her with his shoulder. "And old Bobby is proving himself as capable as any woman, right?"

She nudged his shoulder in return before she turned her attention to her mother.

"Your grandmother said she stood on the porch and watched Hazel take away a tobacco barn."

"On the porch?"

"Yes," her mother said, sounding amazed. "I'm surprised she didn't get blown into the next county — particularly if the winds were anything like this."

"That's exactly why so many people died back then. At least now the forecasters can warn people in plenty of time to take shelter."

The old house creaked and groaned with the incessant winds. Torrential downpours seemed never ending. The deejay spoke of the spotting of tornadoes, adding something else to worry about. Liza certainly didn't need to add that experience to the night.

"Thanks for letting me stay," Lee said. "I don't think I'd want to be in my apartment right now."

"I wouldn't want you to be there alone," Liza told him.

The candles reflected the satisfied light that came into Lee's eyes.

Lord, please help me remain strong, Liza prayed silently. She knew she couldn't change people. She was proof positive of that. Until she had decided to lose the weight, she told herself she was as God intended. She carried the extra pounds, at times hating the restrictions they placed on her physically and mentally. Once she made up her mind, nothing could stop her from achieving her goal. She wished she could say the words to convince Lee to change his life to one of service to the Lord. She could plant the seed, but only God could grow it to greatness.

As the night deepened, the resonant snores of her dad and the gentler ones of her mom could be heard. "Glad they can sleep," she whispered to Lee. "Maybe we should pull out the sofa for them."

"Those recliners look pretty comfortable."

"They are. I've snoozed in them a few times myself."

"Liza . . ."

"Lee . . ."

"You first."

"No, you."

"We're getting nowhere fast," he whispered.

Liza chuckled softly. "You're right. I appreciate your help today."

They had sunk down into the cushions of the sofa and propped their stocking feet on the coffee table. They sat shoulder to shoulder, whispering in their intimate little world.

"You've been on my mind a lot over the past few days. Ever since that incident last time we were together, in fact."

"I was okay."

"I know. Why do you think we have such volatile fights? Every time we get together, we end up arguing."

"Probably because we both expect more of the other person than they're willing to give."

"What do you expect?"

"Not so much expect as want you to understand," she said. "As a Christian, it's my responsibility to be here for my parents now when they need me most. I love my work, but life sometimes has a way of throwing us curve balls."

"It sure threw me one," he agreed.

"In what way?" Liza asked curiously.

"You."

"Me?"

"Let me finish," he insisted. "I had great expectations when I came here. Uncle John more or less guaranteed that once he retires, his business is mine. He felt it was important that his clients adapt to me so they'd stay when he does retire.

"I hope you realize your value to the firm. There's no way everything could get done, if not for your dedication and intuitiveness. You're more than a fixture in the office. You're the lifeblood. In truth, from the first week we worked together, I knew we were a great team."

"I don't always get the impression you're a team player," Liza admitted, voicing the question that had been on her mind. "For instance, why did you choose to live in a hotel instead of Mr. Wilson's home? They would have loved having you there."

"I knew they planned to travel and didn't want the added responsibility of their house. Plus, I didn't care to rattle about alone in that big old place."

He makes sense, Liza thought.

"Besides, I like my privacy," he admitted. "I haven't lived with my parents since I was eighteen. No offense, Liza. I didn't mean

. . . ," he muttered. "Well, it's different for a young, single woman."

"You think so?" she asked. There were times when a place of her own sounded wonderful, but Liza accepted the fact that she needed to be with her parents.

"And I like living on my own."

I bet you do, she thought glumly. A good-looking single man like Lee would never want elderly chaperones.

"Our arguments have a deeper foundation than work. My need for your presence goes far beyond the office. I know you have to be here for your parents, and I'm impressed with the way you've pulled things together.

"Take Kit, for instance. She couldn't have done what you've done this summer. Had the situation arisen, I'm not even sure she would have tried; but you did, and while I've been critical and made some accusations I shouldn't have, the truth of the matter is, my main frustration has been missing having you around.

"We were doing pretty well there at the beginning, but then things started to change. I decided too many changes wouldn't make a good impression on the clients. If Uncle John stepped out of the picture, I at least needed you to make them comfortable. Then things started to change.

I know exactly when it happened: the moment I began seeing you as Liza the woman instead of Liza the coworker. That time you accused me of thinking the office was more important than your happiness was really a time I was afraid Rick would steal you away."

She couldn't help feeling shocked. Lee was so off base. "Rick's a very good friend, but this is the first time I've seen him since I was fourteen."

"You were a young teen then. Now you're a beautiful woman. He looks at you differently."

"We don't feel that way about each other," she protested.

"He could, with very little prompting on your part."

Lee shrugged and admitted, "You're very important to me. And not because you can run the office with one hand tied behind your back. I've fallen in love with you, Liza Stephens."

A tree limb banged on the house, and Liza jumped, realizing the storm raging inside caused the surge of emotion.

"Lee . . ."

He squeezed her hand. "Go ahead, I've had my say."

Liza feared she wasn't strong enough to

withstand after what he'd told her. "Lord, guide me," she whispered fervently. "I love you, too, but there's a problem — a reason we're not ready to advance this relationship." The candlelight played off his frown. Liza forced herself to say what must be said.

"I'm a Christian. I pray for God's guidance in my life, then do my best to accept the answers He gives me. One thing my Bible tells me is that I cannot choose a man who doesn't share my beliefs. In order for a home to prosper and love to grow, two people have to be of the same mind about everything, including their beliefs. I want my children to know my strength comes from above. I want them to share that strength, and I want the man I love to avail himself of it as well."

"I could change."

"I don't want you to change," she objected, struggling to keep her voice down. "I want you to accept Christ as your Savior, but not because it's what I want. I can't get you a place in heaven, and salvation without commitment is meaningless. You need to experience what it means to turn your life over to God."

"Does this mean that I'm going to lose you?"

"No," came her emphatic response.

"Daddy is getting stronger every day and hopefully, by the fall, he'll be capable of handling some of the day-to-day work. Chances are, he'll have to pare down his activities considerably, but we should be able to continue as before."

"What about the farm? Won't it be too stressful for him?"

"The doctor said Daddy's surgery added years to his life."

"No, I meant what do you plan to do . . . ?" Lee began, stopping when her dad spoke.

"Still bad?" Paul Stephens asked, stretching his arms as he came more fully awake.

"Hasn't stopped raining yet," Liza said.

He grunted his frustration.

"How are you feeling?" she asked. "Is it time for your medicine?"

"I'm fine. Don't fuss over me." He glanced over at his wife, watching her doze peacefully. "Your mother does enough of that."

They shared a knowing smile.

"So, Lee, how are you liking our area?"

"I'm getting used to it. Finding that most people are as rooted to the area as their crops."

Paul chuckled. "They believe in hard work. Farming's no playtime operation."

Lee and her father discussed farming and

investments in new machinery and technology.

"None of this newfangled laborsaving equipment can operate itself."

"That's true."

"A lot of it is expertise gained through trial and error spanning generations of farming," her father said. "Most farmers are born and bred to the life."

"Of course, not everyone's cut out to be a farmer." Lee flashed Liza a meaningful look.

Her father nodded agreement. "It's a career of choice. You two had better try to get some sleep. I suspect tomorrow is going to be a busy day."

CHAPTER 13

They left the house at the crack of dawn, feeling like prisoners released from extended exile. Curious and afraid, they went out to determine the extent of the damage. The day dawned clear. A lingering breeze reminded them of the night. Water like never before greeted them.

Both she and her mother argued that her father needed to stay inside and let Liza report to him, but Paul Stephens insisted he needed to see for himself. He promised not to go far.

Liza glanced at her father, afraid the situation might be more than he could bear. Lee noted her concern and stepped to his other side.

"It's gone," he whispered, drooping like the soon-to-be-drowned crops.

"Daddy?" Fear clutched Liza. So much had happened to him over the past couple of months. Could he withstand yet another shock? She slid her arm about his waist and prayed softly, "Please, Jesus, give us strength."

"Amen," he agreed. "I need to climb up to the second floor in the pack house."

"Daddy, no," Liza exclaimed. "You can't."

"I have to see."

"I'll do it. Just stay here."

Liza scurried to the upper floor and threw open the double doors. As a child, she'd sat and dreamed in this loft, but today the dreams of her father's farm plummeted as she surveyed the flooded acreage.

Crops stood in water as far as the eye could see. Tears stung her lids. She glanced at Lee when he came to join her.

"Oh, Lee," she whispered, turning her head against his chest when he wrapped his arms about her.

"Honey, I'm sorry."

"I had no idea it would be this bad."

"You'll have a better idea once the waters recede."

"The damage is already done."

"The government sets aside money for this. I'm sure FEMA will assess the damage quickly. The governor will probably declare this a disaster area within the next couple of days."

Her father's roar caught their attention.

"You have to tell him," Lee urged.

Liza slowly walked down the stairs, trying to formulate the words to soften the blow. How much more could her father take? His hopeful look broke her heart. "It's bad."

His bones seemed to give way to the overwhelming defeat. "Tell me."

She wrapped her arms about him. "It's like a gigantic lake — water as far as I can see. The corn blew over. The vegetables, cotton, and soybeans are standing in the water. I'm sorry."

He stayed silent for several minutes as he continued to hold on to her. "We've been blessed over the years never to have the flooding and total devastation others endured," he said finally.

Lee stood on the sidelines, looking surprised by his reaction. "How can you speak of blessings?"

"We're alive, son. Our house may have a tree lying on the roof, but it's still standing."

"So that's where Liza gets it from."

"Gets what?" her father asked curiously.

"Her ability to see blessings at the worst of times."

Paul Stephens shook his head. "I can't take credit for that. It comes from her faith in the Lord."

"You should go back inside, Daddy. Mom will be worried sick." Barney barked, and Majesty joined in with a neigh of his own, protesting their confines. "I'll check the animals."

"They hear us out here," Dad said. "Don't let Barney out in this mud."

Liza scrutinized her dad's progress. His step was a bit slower than before, but she knew he would survive because that was what farmers had done for hundreds of years. They faced adversity head-on, and with God's more-than-able assistance, farmers came out victorious more times than not.

"I can't believe it's this calm and normal now," Lee said.

She picked up a branch from one of the old pecan trees and dragged it to the side of the yard. "That's the way of a hurricane. Except for the damage, you'd never know the storm had come. Then the assessment and cleanup begins. Given the damage I see here, I'm afraid this is going to be one costly storm."

"What about the tree on the house?"

"Mom will call the agent. Probably would help if we can get it down to check the damage. I wonder if the phone's working. Last time we lost electricity and telephone."

"What about the roads? You think they're flooded?"

"Probably. I'm sure the ditches are over-flowing into the roadway. Those dirt roads will be muddy. Looks like you're stuck with us for a while longer."

"Can't think of any place I'd rather be."

Liza longed to throw her arms about his neck. Instead, she reached for another branch.

Lee grabbed another and said, "I hope the phone's working. I need to call my parents. My mother worries."

"Don't they all? Where's your cell phone?"

"At the apartment. I let the battery go dead. In all the rush, I walked off and left it at home."

Rick and Dave showed up later that morning in one of their big, expensive tractors. Mud caked the huge wheels. Dave opened the cab door and climbed down. Rick followed. "Glad to see you made it okay. Kit's ready to get out of the house. I told her to stay put."

"I wouldn't be surprised to see her show up on horseback," Liza told him.

"I don't think she's thought of that yet. Maybe I should borrow a white horse and go to her rescue," Dave teased. "Nah, he'd be brown with mud and probably break a leg, to boot. We're headed over that way next."

"You shouldn't have come out."

"It's our spirit of adventure, the need to explore."

Liza eyed Rick skeptically. "The need to get yourself pinned under a tractor? Possibly even drowned?"

"We're in contact with the house," Dave said, reminding Liza of their two-way radio. "Besides, we know Dad will skin us alive if we mess up his tractor. That's plenty of incentive to be careful."

"Is it as bad as I think?" Liza hoped to hear things were different elsewhere.

Rick nodded his head. "The entire state is reporting flooding like you wouldn't believe. The river won't crest for days yet, and we're already in trouble. Twenty-one inches of rain fell in less than twenty-four hours. Looked pretty bad from what I saw on Mom's battery-operated television. Your mom said there's a tree on the house. We bought the chain saw to get it down for you."

Liza appreciated the fact that they were willing to help their neighbors. Given the size of their farm, no doubt they had plenty to do at their place. "Thanks, guys."

Rick hefted the saw from the tractor and glanced at Lee. "You want to help?"

The men seemed intent on measuring each other up from a distance. Lee stepped forward. "Tell me what to do."

"Grab a ladder from the barn."

"I'll show you where it is," Liza offered. She forgot about Barney, and when she opened the door, the dog charged outside, knocking her into a nearby mud puddle.

The three men laughed heartily at her plight as they dodged the dog. Barney ran from person to person, slinging mud as he allowed them to pet him. "Exactly why was it you wanted that dog?" Dave asked, reaching down to offer a hand.

Liza refused to comment. "The ladder's in the corner. I'm going to change."

Barney trailed after Liza to the house, keeping his distance.

By the time she returned, Rick was on the roof, and a rope dangled with the chain saw attached.

"Everyone stand clear," he yelled. The powerful roar of the saw echoed throughout the area, the volume changing as he worked his way through branch after branch and dropped them to the ground. Once Rick removed the top of the tree, he killed the saw and leaned over the edge.

"Doesn't appear to have damaged more than the overhang. We can tack down a tarp until the insurance adjuster comes. Watch out. I'm going to see if I can move this trunk."

Luckily, it wasn't one of their biggest trees and with a mighty heave, he shoved the remaining trunk of the tree from the house. It hit the ground with a thump, falling just short of the shrubbery.

"Here comes the saw," he called.

Dave grabbed the saw and started it again, carving the trunk into smaller pieces.

Rick climbed down the ladder and walked over to where Liza stood. "What's he doing here?" he asked in an undertone, nodding his head in Lee's direction.

"I invited him."

Rick's brows raised.

"He lives in an apartment. Besides, he was a lot of help yesterday."

"You're going to get hurt."

"No, she's not."

Liza jumped when Lee spoke from right behind her. "We have an understanding," he told Rick, glancing at Liza when he said, "I love Liza, and I would never intentionally do anything to hurt her."

Rick glanced from one to the other.

"Good. I don't care to see anyone break my friend's heart. Let's clean up this mess."

CHAPTER 14

On Sunday morning, Liza looked out from the choir loft into the sea of faces and was surprised when Lee waved at her. She smiled back and nodded her head slightly.

Why is he here? Surely he isn't attending church to change my mind? The thought upset her so much that she couldn't even remember the words of the song. She wasn't being fair. Lee wasn't that kind of person. Liza forced her attention back to the service.

Afterward she shed her robe and hurried out to find him chatting with her parents.

He kissed her cheek. "How are you doing?"

His welcoming smile filled an empty place in her heart. "Fine. It's been a busy time, though."

"Getting everything sorted out okay?"

"Sure. What about you? Rhonda told me about the mess at the office."

"Maybe a foot of water entered the building. We had to strip out the carpet. One of the file cabinets burst from the force of the wet paper. I've never seen anything like it."

"Anything important?"

"Copies of old invoices. Thankfully no client files. No great loss."

Her parents said good-bye to Lee and walked over to speak to their friends. "I'm glad you came today," Liza said, pushing aside her earlier doubts.

Lee reached for her hand. "I enjoy being here. I saw an angel in the choir this morning."

His regard was almost embarrassing. "Are you flattering me to get an invitation to lunch?"

"Would it work?"

"Probably."

"Actually Uncle John and Aunt Clara are expecting me. I wanted to say hello. Could we go out to dinner one night soon?"

"I'll see. Kit's had me so busy with plans for this wedding of hers. Four more weeks and it'll be over. I can tell you this much: I think I'll be as happy to see them off on their honeymoon as they will be to go!"

"You won't say the same when it's your turn." Lee flashed her a knowing smile. "Do you have an escort for Kitty's wedding?"

"Not really, but I suppose I'll be too busy

anyway."

"We'll discuss it later." He kissed her cheek and waved good-bye to her parents.

Despite her efforts to restrain herself, Liza's hope grew with each passing week as Lee continued to meet her at church. He attended faithfully on Wednesday nights and Sundays. He enrolled in the Thursday night Bible study class, which surprised her, given how busy he was at work. She knew from experience that the course was no lightweight study.

"Want to go for ice cream?" he asked after the group disbanded.

The subject that had been troubling her came to mind. Seemed like as good a time as any to discuss the matter. "Sure."

The little shop's popularity made it a difficult place to talk. Several people tried to beat the heat with a cone of their favorite flavor. Liza and Lee stood in line, Liza opting for a tropical-flavored yogurt while Lee chose chocolate ice cream.

"This is good. Want to taste?" She held out her cone.

"No, thanks. Chocolate is my flavor. Let's sit outside."

They found a bench and enjoyed the late August night.

Lee caught the melting ice cream running down his cone with a swipe of his tongue. "I'm really enjoying this Bible class."

Liza licked her frozen yogurt and asked, "When do you find time to study?"

"Early in the morning. At night after I get home. Don't tell Uncle John, but the Bible has replaced my briefs."

The revelation surprised her, but then God was in the miracle business. "You've slowed down a bit."

Brilliant blue eyes focused on her. "Now that a particular lady has stolen my heart, I've found other interests."

His openness about his feelings stole her breath away. Liza could hardly believe he loved her. "Lee? I need to ask you something. Please don't take this the wrong way," she pleaded, "but I wonder about your church attendance. You aren't . . ."

"Attending because of you?"

He didn't answer, just stood and walked over to the trash can to dispose of his napkin and the remainder of his cone.

Feeling she'd made a serious mistake, Liza wiped her sticky fingers and balled the napkin tightly in her hand. She walked over to his side and dropped her trash into the can. "I've offended you, haven't I?"

He looked at her and shook his head. "No.

It's not what you think."

"I don't understand."

"I like what I feel in your presence, what I hear coming from your lips. You're spiritually grounded, and you don't center on yourself."

In the past, her focus on her emotions had caused her to treat him badly. "I wouldn't go that far."

"I would. Ready?" Lee took her hand as they walked toward the car. After helping her inside, he came around and sat in the driver's seat. "My relationship with God has been too long in coming. I believe He put you in my life for this reason — to open my eyes. I was afraid you might think my newfound need for religion had to do with your ultimatum."

"No, Lee. I never meant it as an ultimatum."

"Well, you should have. A woman needs a committed man. My devotion to the almighty dollar didn't give me much comfort. Possessions just don't fill the void. And I'm finally accepting the void. I searched for years but was never able to give a name to the emptiness.

"When I left Charlotte, someone told me a big-city lawyer couldn't be happy in a small town. Boy, were they wrong. I've never been happier. Never felt more fulfilled. I'm not fooling myself, though. For the first time in my life, I know I'm on the right track spiritually. I've reprioritized my life."

"Thank God," Liza said, her eyes drifting closed as she drew a deep breath. "I want you to know Christ as your Savior for all the right reasons."

He leaned to kiss her cheek. "I know. Believe me, I'd never try to fool you into believing I was something I'm not."

"I'd better get home. Mom and Dad will worry about me."

"How about that dinner?"

"I'll call you soon and set a date."

Time had a way of getting away from her as Liza worked around the farm, trying to salvage what she could of their crops. A week before the wedding, Kit showed up at the house on Saturday afternoon and found Liza working in the garden.

"What are you doing out here alone?"

"Hoeing." Liza grinned at her friend. Her mother had planted a late garden, and it was doing well. The weeds, in particular, flourished. She didn't add that she needed the private time for reflection. In time she'd confide the truth, but not now.

"I can see that, silly. Why isn't your mom

helping?"

"She did until lunchtime. Daddy's not feeling well. I suggested she stay inside with him. Even with those tests, the surgery, and medication, we're still nervous about his heart condition."

"Want some help?"

"Sure. How's life treating you?"

Kitty pulled a handful of weeds and tossed them to the side. "Can't complain. It's hot. I'll be glad to see fall."

Liza's face creased in a grin. "Thought you couldn't complain?"

"I've been working hard. I do believe everybody in town has been to the office this week. I didn't think farmers had time to be sick."

"They don't exactly have a choice in the matter."

Kitty took her time, careful not to damage her manicured nails. Liza dared not offer her a hoe, or she'd be sporting blisters at her wedding.

Her own hands were rough, her nails chipped. *I could do with a manicure.* Liza promised herself one as soon as work slacked off to the point where it would be worthwhile — definitely before the wedding next week. Meanwhile, she would find time to file her nails and put lotion on her hands.

"You didn't mention the late-afternoon thunderstorms."

"Dave's having a time because of them. They've been running behind all week. He all but stood me up last night."

Liza glanced up, curiosity lighting her eyes. "What happened?"

"We were supposed to go to a movie, but he didn't get to the house until almost nine. He was so tired I hated to insist, so we just sat on the porch and talked."

"And?"

"Don't be so nosy," Kitty said, wrinkling her nose at Liza. "Dave's a wonderful man. We have so much in common."

Liza feigned surprise. "Really?"

"Rub it in," Kitty said good-naturedly. "I know you've been saying we'd get together for years. He's perfect for me. Of course, he is a farmer. That part's not great, but I suppose things could be worse."

Liza froze at her friend's comments. "You wouldn't try to talk him into doing something else?"

"Don't be silly. Liza, I recognize the hints you've been dropping. I've lived around farmers long enough to know you can't change them. If the land makes Dave happy, I'm okay with it. I love Dave Evans enough that I'd rather have a few minutes a day of his time than nothing."

"I doubt it'll be a few minutes," Liza said, the tension easing from her body. "Wedding plans under control?"

"Finally. We've got the group down to a manageable number, and come next Sunday afternoon, I'll say 'I do' to the man of my dreams."

The man of her dreams. How Liza longed to say those words herself. In her heart and mind, Lee fit the position perfectly, but their relationship was far from Kit and Dave's happy beginning.

"Sorry I can't stick around and help you finish, but Dave promised to come by tonight and help with the birdseed packets."

"I'm glad you stopped by." Liza hugged her, tears stinging her eyes as she watched Kitty run for her car, carried along in the euphoria only true love could bring. She turned back to the row that seemed to stretch forever.

Even though she was happy for Kitty, envy kept interfering with the excitement she should be feeling. She didn't want to feel this way.

Rick stopped by on Wednesday. Refusing her offer to come inside, he remained in the truck. He handed her a small brown paper sack of boiled peanuts he'd picked up at the tobacco warehouse. "Dave said you love these things. Don't know why. I can't stand them."

"They're an acquired taste," Liza explained, unrolling the top of the small bag. "How are things over at your house? Getting crazy?"

"Mom and Kit's mom keep trying to make changes to their plans. Last night Dave warned Mom to stop or they'll elope."

"Doesn't sound like Dave."

"Mom didn't think so either. She was still fussing this morning. Blamed Kitty, but what she doesn't realize is, her baby has become his own man. She'll have another fit when she learns they're fixing up a house near Kitty's father's place."

"Where did she think they were going to stay?"

"At the house, I guess. She'll be lost when we leave."

Liza stopped shelling the peanut and looked at Rick. "You're leaving? When?"

"Sunday night. I've got to get back to England. Kit and Dave are going, too. Tell me I'm not a glutton for punishment."

Liza leaned against the truck, crossing her arms in the open window. "Why didn't you tell me earlier?"

"I planned to. There's been so much going on."

She pasted on a smile. Everything was changing so fast. "Well, I guess I'll see you Sunday." Liza pushed herself away from the truck.

"Liza, wait." His fingers closed about her arm. "I don't suppose I should expect you to cry every time I leave?"

She touched his hand. "You can if you insist on waltzing in and out of my life every fourteen years. Seriously, though, I want you to do the things that make you happy. I'm not the same child I was all those years ago. I know you're cut out for greatness, and I'm glad you have the guts to go after it."

His smile widened in approval. "You're some woman, Liza Stephens. When do you go after what you really want?"

She knew exactly what he meant. "When God says it's time."

"It's going to happen, Liza. I know you love Lee, and he loves you. God brought you two together for a reason."

"I believe that, Rick. I'm seeing a real difference in Lee. He's attending church, and I know he's going to turn his life over to God one day soon. He may not realize it yet, but he's already changed from the man he was when we first met."

"Love has a way of doing that to a guy," Rick said. "I see it in Dave's eyes when he looks at Kitty, and I see it in Lee's eyes when he looks at you. One day soon I hope to have others see it in my eyes when I look at the woman I love."

"You will."

Sunday dawned beautifully clear — not a dark cloud in the sky, not on Kitty's wedding day. Thinking of all the things she needed to be doing before the wedding, Liza considered missing church, but the feeling she needed to attend was strong.

She missed Sunday school but managed to pull into the parking lot shortly before the eleven o'clock service. Looking around for Lee's car, she spotted it on the far side of the lot. It was too late to get into her choir robe, so she decided to sit this one out. The opening hymn began as she headed for the pew. Lee glanced up and waved for her to join him.

He shared the hymnal with her. Liza felt so happy standing by his side, experiencing the little things couples did for each other. The hour passed quickly. The pastor preached a stirring sermon on love, reminding them how powerful God's love was for each and every one of them.

During the altar call, Liza sang the hymn from memory, her mind wandering to her list of things to do before she went to Kitty's. It took her a second to realize Lee had left the pew. Surprised, she looked up to find him talking with the pastor up front.

Joy greater than anything she'd ever known burst forth in her heart, and tears of delight filled her eyes. He and the pastor bowed their heads as the choir and congregation continued to sing. Liza's voice rose in volume at the wonder of the moment.

"Ladies and gentlemen," the pastor said, standing before them with Lee by his side. "Lee Hayden has come forth today to make a profession of faith. He plans to follow up his commitment with believer's baptism and a request to join our church. Please step forward and extend the right hand of fellowship to him today."

Liza knew she hardly had any time before she was expected at Kit's. She needed to go home and pick up her dress. Still, there was no way she would walk out of church today without sharing her joy with Lee.

Never had a line moved so slowly. By the time she reached Lee, she had few minutes to spare. Her handshake turned into a hug, and she smiled, her eyes watery with tears of elation. "I love you," she whispered, smiling when he lowered one lid in a conspiratorial wink. "I can't stay. Kit's going to kill me if I don't get over there now."

"Can't have her doing that. Go. I'll see you at the wedding."

"Where have you been?" Kitty demanded when Liza stepped into the bedroom. "Where are my hose? I won't ever be ready in time."

After knowing Kit for so long, Liza thought she knew every facet of her personality, but she'd never seen Kitty panic before. Good thing Kitty didn't get married every day; Liza doubted her nerves could take it. "So they'll wait. You're the star of the show," she comforted. "Settle down. You're doing fine."

Liza was glad she'd decided to dress at home. Kitty had chosen a very classy dress for her, insisting there was no reason for them not to be dolled up. Two pieces, the lace top had a scalloped neckline and a tiered georgette skirt stopped about mid-calf. The lilac color complemented Liza's dark hair and tan.

Kitty refused to let her pay for the dress, insisting she cover the cost herself because she had only one attendant. Liza felt it had more to do with her being out of work and explained she was still being paid, but her obstinate friend refused to budge, so Liza finally gave in.

"I've got flowers for your hair," Kitty said, going over to sort through the bouquets to find them.

They tucked the tiny white rosebuds and baby's breath in place in her dark curls. Liza looked in the mirror and nodded. "Everything's perfect. I can't believe you did all this in a couple of months."

"Me neither. Did I tell you Daddy finished my gazebo?" Kitty continued to touch up her makeup.

After a great deal of argument, Kitty's parents had accepted her plans to turn her wedding into an outside event. Any sort of ceremony with relatives and friends was preferable to missing their only daughter's wedding. "He's going to take it to our house after the wedding. He painted it white, and I got ferns and ribbons. It's pretty, even if I do say so."

"Did you call the photographer?"

"He promised to be here on time. Oh, Liza, I'm so scared and excited. Dave called earlier to tell me he loves me. Sometimes I just can't believe it's happening."

After Lee's decision, Liza couldn't help

but hope there was a future for them. She didn't want to take anything away from her friend's day, but the need to share the news overwhelmed her.

"Liza, that's wonderful," Kitty exclaimed, hugging her.

"I left him standing at the altar to get over here."

"I'm sorry. I know what a struggle that must have been."

Liza picked up the wedding gown from the bed. "I didn't want to leave. Let's get you into this so I can see him again."

"Hey, slow down, girl," Kitty said. "If he's worth having, he's worth waiting for. Besides, I'm trying to stretch these minutes into memories to last a lifetime."

Kitty had gone the whole nine yards with her dress. "A girl only gets married once," she said when they visited the bridal shop. She'd stood on the pedestal, looking every inch the perfect bride and asked, "It'll be fine, won't it?"

The question surprised Liza. Kitty was a confident person, always so certain of what she wanted. "You like it, don't you?" she'd asked.

"Love it."

"Then that's all that matters."

As Kitty slipped the bishop sleeves over

her arms and smoothed the lace-draped neckline into place, Liza almost cried. Even the plainest girl made a beautiful bride, but Kitty looked like a fairy princess. Dave would never forget the vision she made when she walked down the aisle to meet him.

"Button me. Mom had a fit about this," she said, indicating the full-tiered lace chapel train. "I took care of that, though. Jason agreed to pull a runner over the grass just before the ceremony."

After posturing to get a better reflection in the mirror, Kit picked up the Victorian lace collar and passed it to her. "Help me with this. I'm all thumbs."

Liza stood behind her friend, looking at her in the mirror. "You're beautiful."

"We make quite a picture," Kitty agreed. "Promise you'll always be my best friend."

"Always."

The last thing was her veil. Liza fitted the lace cap over Kit's shining blond curls and pinned it carefully. "You want this in place now?" She held out the netting.

"What time is it?"

"The photographer is waiting to take pictures. By the time he finishes, it'll be time for the wedding march."

"You'd better get Mom and Dad."

The photographer took his shots, and Liza picked up their flowers, leaving Kitty for a few private moments with her parents.

From the window, she watched the guests assemble in the garden. Clearly Kitty and Dave failed in their attempt to curb the number. Nobody wanted to miss this wedding.

Kitty appeared at her side. "Looks like we're playing to a packed house."

"You should have charged admission," Liza teased, moving Kit's blusher veil into place. "Where's your father?"

"He's coming. Poor Daddy," Kit sympathized. "I still think he wants to lock me in my room instead of walk me down the aisle."

"Probably. Remember, I was there when he said you couldn't date until you were thirty." Liza kissed her cheek and squeezed her hand before putting the bouquet into Kitty's hand. "I love you. Be happy."

There were tears in both women's eyes as they walked out of the house. Liza moved down the aisle, smiling at Dave and Rick when she took her place on the opposite side.

Dave's expression spoke volumes when Kitty came forward. Another picture came to Liza's mind. She pushed it away. All in

God's time. He'd already worked a miracle. She couldn't hope for more now.

The vows rang in her ears and in a fight to regain her composure, Liza allowed her gaze to touch on the crowd. A tiny smile touched her lips when she spotted Lee in the group. His grin was huge as he mouthed, "I love you."

"Liza," Kitty whispered, "the ring." Bringing her attention back to her duties, Liza found the item in question and placed it in her friend's hand.

Within minutes, Kitty became Mrs. David Evans. After a photo session, the wedding party entered the tent where the guests awaited them. This time Liza greeted guests in the receiving line.

"We seem to be waiting in line to see each other today," Lee said when he finally got to her. "You look beautiful."

"Thank you. Wasn't it a pretty wedding?"

"Very. We need to talk."

"Liza, the photographer wants to take more photos," Kitty called. "Sorry. I didn't realize you were talking to Lee."

"Save me a cup of punch," Liza told him, waving good-bye as she continued her attendant duties.

The next couple of hours were filled with picture taking, cake cutting, helping Kitty change, and entertaining guests. Several times, Liza found herself headed in Lee's direction, only to have her plans upset. They waved the newlyweds off to Dave's decorated car in a flurry of birdseed.

"Think the cans are a bit much?" Rick asked, grinning as they clattered down the highway.

"The shaving cream and toilet tissue would have been enough," Liza said.

She had vetoed his suggestion of packing the couple's luggage with confetti, reminding him of the mandatory payback they would set themselves up for as the remaining singles.

"Miss her already?"

She turned to face Lee, her dress whispering with the movement. Rick disappeared.

"She'll be back."

He brushed birdseed from her hair. "How did you manage that?" he asked, pointing to Kitty's bouquet.

"It helps to have your best friend as the bride. She all but put it into my hands."

He grinned and reached into his pocket. The blue-beribboned garter dangled from his index finger. "She must have instructed Dave to make sure I got this."

"Probably." Liza giggled at the thought.

"Would you like to attend church services

with me tonight?"

She turned his arm to check his watch. There was just enough time to get home and change clothes. "I'll meet you at church."

"Why don't I go with you and visit with your parents while you change?"

"Let me get my things."

After talking with Kitty's mom and finding things were under control, Liza headed across the yard to her car.

She stopped when Rick came out of the house, calling her name. "I'm leaving early in the morning to meet Dave and Kit at the airport to fly to London. I wanted to say good-bye and tell you it's been wonderful seeing you again this summer."

"I'll miss you. Don't be a stranger."

Rick wrapped his arms about her and said, "I'm praying for you and your family."

"Liza?"

They glanced at Lee.

"Coming. Stay in touch, Rick."

"You, too. I'll be praying for you and Lee. God bless."

She kissed his cheek. "I'm praying for you, too."

CHAPTER 15

Three weeks later, Liza bleakly surveyed the mess before her, knowing there was enough work to keep her busy for more than the day she allotted. Served her right. She should have had better sense than to start such a job. The barn hadn't been cleaned properly in years. Stubborn determination made her push on with the latest of her keep-busy tasks.

It wasn't really necessary, but neither were the other jobs she'd done in the past few days. Thanks to Hurricane Bobby, the majority of their harvest had been a bounty of paperwork. They had managed to get a few fall crops in the ground, but it would be awhile before they began to produce.

Her father was doing much better — so much so, Dr. Mayes released him the day before, saying that if her dad exercised his leg, he wouldn't have a limp. The heart condition was something he would have to accept, but he could live a normal life.

He worked, but Liza insisted that he rest often. She knew he didn't really need her any longer, but she put off making her final decision.

Her life hadn't been the same since Lee Hayden came to her rescue all those months ago, and Liza knew it never would be. She saw him often but was so confused by his behavior. They attended church together, went out to dinner, and Lee often told her he loved her, but he hadn't brought up the subject of marriage.

Liza thought maybe Lee felt he needed to give them time to get used to the idea of being a couple, but now that they seemed to be comfortable in each other's company, his hurry had slowed down to a crawl.

"A woman's work is never done."

"Kit!" She whirled about, dropping the bucket and hurrying over to hug her friend. "How's married life, Mrs. Evans?"

"I won't say perfect, but let's say the ups make the downs worthwhile," she teased, appearing lit from inside. "Actually I highly recommend marriage. What about you? Did our subtle hints inspire Lee to propose?"

Crestfallen, Liza's smile quickly faded. "I think he's changed his mind."

Kitty's mouth fell open. "No way."

"I don't know what else to think. He's attending the new-Christian class at church now. We see each other at church fairly often and go out when we can, but that's all."

"I think you're wrong about Lee. If I guessed at a reason, I'd say he's like Dave and me. Adapting to change can be all-consuming. I thought I knew everything about Dave before we married, but I haven't even scratched the surface yet. It'll take another fifty years, I'm sure."

Liza sat on a nearby bale of hay and pulled one leg underneath her. "At least you're committed to figuring him out."

"Don't give up on Lee. I'm sure he never expected to find a relationship with Christ and the woman of his dreams when he came here."

"Maybe not. I just hate this state of limbo. I want more. Tell me about your honeymoon."

Kitty talked for several minutes about London and all they had seen. "Rick was a pretty decent guide. He gave us a quick tour, then we'd get together every couple of days for him to make suggestions on what we should do. Otherwise, he left us alone."

"Doesn't hurt to have someone who knows the area," Liza agreed. "So what are your plans now that you're home?"

"Dave's already deserted me for the land," Kit said. "I'm getting the house organized this week and going back to work next. We've decided to start a family soon."

"Don't you think you should give yourself time to get used to being married first?"

"Neither of us are getting any younger. We both love children. We've decided on at least three. One at a time, of course."

"Wow. Kids."

"Flighty Kitty, huh? I surprise myself in so many ways. It's like I woke up from a deep sleep and found I didn't want to exist without Dave. Funny, don't you think?"

"No. Perfect," Liza whispered. That was the way she felt about Lee.

"I wanted to let you know I was back and give you this," Kitty said, handing Liza a souvenir from London. "I'd better head home to fix Dave's lunch. Me cooking — can you believe it?"

She considered her friend's lack of experience in that area and asked, "What's on the menu?"

"Sandwiches. I'll throw in a can of soup if he's really hungry."

"He must really be in love."

Kit continued to laugh as she walked out the barn door. A new husband and home now kept Kitty busy. Liza missed the times they shared.

Right now she didn't feel she could talk to anyone about her feelings. She couldn't bring herself to voice her fears to her parents, not with them having so many problems of their own. Things were finally looking up for them. They didn't need her dragging them into her despair.

And in truth, she was afraid not even the open, honest relationship she shared with them, trusting them as friends and confidants, could handle this one. Deep down, she prayed her doubts would go away.

Hunger gnawed at her empty stomach. According to Kit, it was lunchtime. Liza strolled toward the house. *The yard needs to be mowed,* she thought, noting yet another task to be completed.

She stopped to wash up. The water from the faucet on the back porch was cold against her skin. Lathering her hands heavily with soap, Liza scrubbed vigorously to wash away the morning's grime, wishing desperately that she could do the same with her thoughts.

Liza cupped her hands, filling them with water before tossing it onto her face. The coolness unsettled her lethargic state, and in quick, jerky movements, she tugged a towel from the rack and dried her face and hands. The screen door slammed shut with a bang behind her.

Her father was seated at the table, studying one of his favorite farm journals while her mother moved about the stove, spooning the vegetables into serving bowls.

"What's for lunch?"

"Fried chicken."

Liza looked at the plate holding a couple of pieces of golden bird her mother placed in front of her. The other plate held baked chicken. "You didn't have to go to all that trouble. I could have eaten baked."

"I wanted to do something special for you. Oh, here's a letter," her mother said, pulling the envelope from her apron pocket. "Very fancy. Engraved and everything."

Liza noted the Wilsons' address and laid it aside.

"Aren't you going to open it?" her mother asked.

"Later."

She bowed her head while her dad said grace and reached for the salad bowl in the center of the table.

"Open it, Liza," her mother encouraged.

Taking a deep, steadying breath, Liza picked up the envelope and snapped the seal with her finger. Quickly scanning the contents, she dropped it to the table. "Mr. Wilson's retirement party."

The news came as no surprise to her. Lee had everything he'd worked for, thanks to his uncle. Liza found the reality unsettling. Even though she'd known this was coming, now she found herself worrying about the future. Could she work for the man she loved? Picking up her fork, Liza made a desultory attempt to eat her meal.

"How nice," her mother enthused, shaking out her napkin as she settled into her chair. "When is it?"

"Didn't you open your invitation, Mom?"

Sarah Stephens set the bowl on the table with a thump. "I hoped you'd talk to us again. You've shut us out of your life."

Liza pushed her chair back from the table. She glanced at her father, sensing his concern and knowing he wouldn't interfere. He would be there when she was ready to talk. That was all he could do. "I'm sorry. I don't mean to. It's just that I'm trying to sort out my life right now. Excuse me, please."

"Liza, honey, wait," her mother called, her voice strained.

Liza stood frozen in the doorway. She loathed herself for hurting the two dearest people in the world.

The chair scraped as it slid backward, followed by the whisper of her mother's slippers across the linoleum floor. Her hand rested on Liza's shoulder. "Never deal with anything alone. Talk with God. He can provide the answer. And promise me you'll attend this party."

Liza shrugged, pushing hurriedly out the door. "We'll see, Mom. We'll see."

She went into the barn and started the mower in hopes of taking her mind off the incident. But as the mower cut a swath through the grass, her thoughts continued to bother Liza. God waited for her to ask what He wanted for her instead of what she wanted for herself. As usual, she selfishly orchestrated her life to her own specifications, not praying for answers. She'd decided that Lee would be perfect for her if he was saved, but had God?

She was a hypocrite. All those times she'd accused Lee of being selfish, of looking out only for himself, and she did the same thing. The realization jarred her. Liza mowed the path around the curve where her parents couldn't see her and turned off the mower. She sat in the silence and, for the first time in weeks, opened her heart to the Author and Finisher of her faith.

"How's my girl?" Lee asked later that

evening when he called.

"Good. And you?"

"Busy." He launched into a description of his life for the past few days. "What time should I pick you up for Uncle John's party?"

The way he took it for granted bothered Liza, but her prayer sessions helped her curb her tongue. If God planned something for Lee and her, Liza would await His answer. "I thought you called to ask when I planned to come back to work."

"We can discuss it at the party."

"You promised no business on our dates."

"If you insist on holding me to a promise made under duress . . ."

"I do," Liza said. "Pick me up at six thirty."

Liza spent the hours while she worked thinking about what she would wear. She wanted to look good, if only to give her the confidence she needed, and spent intervening days in preparation — some with feverish activity, but always in prayer.

As she applied her makeup, Liza tossed the eyeliner back onto the dresser, her hands too shaky to even try.

At times, she considered their differences — a lawyer and a farmer's daughter — and her doubts resurfaced. Lee didn't understand what this farm meant to her family. "You should just give up before you get hurt," she told the face in the mirror.

Don't, a small, insistent voice deep inside prompted. Where would she be if Jesus Christ had given up?

She twisted her hair up on top of her head and secured it with enameled combs. Slipping on the dress she'd chosen, Liza hoped Lee would be proud of her.

The deep red complemented her dark hair and made her feel feminine. Downstairs, the first person she saw was her mother.

"Liza, you're breathtaking."

"Think so?" she asked, the uncertainty of her thoughts running over into her words.

Silently mother and daughter stood, carefully handling the fragile relationship between them. Liza's feelings were still too raw to discuss, but their love was a tangible thing, strong enough to carry them through any storm.

"Honey, you've always been beautiful to me," her mother assured, her lips curving in an unconscious smile. "From the moment you came into the world," she reminisced. "My precious baby girl."

With a sob, Liza moved into her arms.

"I'm so sorry. I love you and Daddy so much."

Protective arms sheltered her child. "We know. Now stop crying before you ruin your makeup."

With a teary smile, Liza stepped back, sniffling occasionally. Her hand clutched her mother's. Nervously she moistened her lips, trying to swallow the knot of tension that remained. The silence was so absolute even her breathing sounded loud.

"Mom," she whispered, "what do you do when you don't have the slightest idea what the man you love intends?"

A sympathetic smile flitted across her mother's face. "It's hard, isn't it?"

Liza was puzzled by her response.

"Don't look so shocked," her mother said. "I was a reasonably attractive woman in my day."

"Beautiful," Liza corrected.

"I made a decision, too. But when it comes to love, there's no choice to make. I loved your father, and as the only son, he accepted the responsibility. Not that he ever wanted a different life, but he always said no child of his would be pressured into doing something he didn't want to do. That's why I regret not having more children."

"What are you saying, Mom?"

"Wait for Lee. You won't regret it."

"I don't even know what he's thinking."

"Take a chance, Liza. Don't be one of those women who spends her life wishing she had done something."

"Promise me you'll be around to pick up the pieces."

Her mother squeezed her hand, the loving warmth of her smile touching Liza's heart. "Come show your daddy."

They entered the living room together. Her father sat in his recliner, watching his favorite television program.

"Paul," her mother called softly, stepping away from Liza's side. "What do you think of our daughter tonight?"

He glanced sideways, his head snapping back. "Whooee. That boy isn't going to know what hit him," he teased. Slowly he stood, his arms outstretched in loving welcome.

Liza took the steps eagerly, running to him. "I love you," she whispered. No matter what the future held, they would never suffer again because of her, Liza vowed. The doorbell rang, and she smiled at them before going to open the door for Lee.

"Wow."

"Is that all you can say?" she asked, striking a model's pose. "Not too shabby for a farmer's daughter?"

He shook his head. "Not shabby at all."

"You look very handsome tonight." Liza smoothed his expensive silk tie.

He kissed her. Liza led the way into the family room.

"Hello, Lee."

"Hello, Mrs. Stephens, Mr. Stephens. I can see I've got my work cut out for me tonight with this beauty."

"Have fun. We'll see you both later."

"It's going to be a wonderful evening," Lee said, promise lighting the eyes that rested on her when he spoke the words.

The party was in full swing when they arrived at the Wilsons' home. Liza greeted Mr. and Mrs. Wilson, then Lee pulled her farther into the room.

"Mom, Dad, there's someone I want you to meet. Liza Stephens, James and Sheila Hayden, my parents."

Disturbed by his lack of warning, Liza managed a smile and cordial greeting. "Nice to meet you."

"You, too, dear. Lee has told us such wonderful things about you. How are your parents?"

"Fine. They should be here shortly."

His mother beamed at her. "We can hardly

wait to meet them. They've raised a wonderful daughter."

Her praise sounded sincere, but it confused Liza. Lee's mother knew nothing of Liza or her parents. What had Lee told his parents about her? "Thank you. You have a great son."

Lee leaned over to whisper in her ear. "Visit with Mom and Dad a bit. I need to talk with Uncle John in the library. I'll be right back."

"But, Lee," she objected. Already he'd forgotten his no-business promise.

He patted her arm. "You'll be fine. This will only take a few minutes."

Her pride took a beating when it came to holding Lee's attention for any length of time. She considered it unfair of him not to warn her, but on the other hand, common sense told her they'd be there.

"So, Mr. and Mrs. Hayden, how are you enjoying our little community?" she asked, afraid her efforts to make conversation were stilted at best.

Lee's mother smiled. "Call us Sheila and Jim. I lived here until I went off to college. We prefer larger cities."

Real smart, Liza thought. *I knew that.* "I've never lived anywhere but here."

"After you and Lee . . ." Lee's father

touched his wife's arm and shook his head slightly. "So how long have you worked for John?" she asked instead.

"Since I graduated from high school."

Sheila Hayden's animated gestures reminded her very much of her son's. "I know John feels you're an asset to the firm."

The woman's flattery made Liza feel uncomfortable. "I was the fortunate one. Mr. Wilson has taught me a lot about law."

"Lee says you should get your degree. Have you ever considered going to law school?"

Lee's mother should be a lawyer. Sophisticated and beautiful, she could cross-examine with the best of them.

Still, Lee's opinion of her ability pleased Liza. "I like what I do. I'm not really courtroom material."

"Liza."

"Kit," she cried, hugging her friend and then Dave. She introduced them to Lee's parents. "This is Dave and Kitty Evans."

"The newlyweds. Lee told us he attended your wedding. I dated your father years ago, Dave. How is he?"

"Great. Busy with the farm."

"Lee mentioned you honeymooned in London."

Obviously Lee enjoyed a better relationship with his parents than she realized. He seemed to have kept them current on everything.

Dave placed his arm about Kitty's waist. "Yes, ma'am, we did."

"We've been to England a couple of times. It's wonderful," Sheila enthused.

"We plan to go back again," Kitty said. "By the way, Liza, Rick called earlier. He sends his love."

"Rick?" Lee's mother asked curiously.

"Dave's brother," Kitty explained. "Our built-in tour guide in London."

"That sounds wonderful. Clara is looking a bit overwhelmed," Sheila told her husband. "You should tell John and Lee to come back to the party."

"I'll go," Liza volunteered.

"Thank you, dear."

She tapped on the study door and opened it. "Mr. Wilson, you really should . . ."

Lee glanced up from the papers he was studying. "Give us a few more minutes, Liza."

His words hit her like a shock of ice water. "Your mom asked me to let Mr. Wilson know Mrs. Wilson needs him out here." Just before she shut the door, she heard Mr. Wilson's chuckle.

"Come on, Lee. We can finish this later.

This party is in my honor. If I want to enjoy my retirement, I'd better show my face."

Piqued by Lee's dismissive attitude, Liza stepped out into the Wilsons' garden and strolled along the beautifully landscaped walkway, trying to work through the growing apprehension she felt.

Why couldn't Lee wait until a better time to talk with his uncle? She settled in the swing and pushed herself back and forth for several minutes.

Realizing pride controlled her, Liza frowned. She needed to go back inside and celebrate with her employer. After all he'd done for her over the years, he deserved her appreciation. Besides, she wanted to see his face when she gave him the hat she had found. She knew, without a doubt, the hat with a big fish through the center would make him laugh.

"There you are."

Looking at Lee, she asked, "Finish your business?"

"We were tying up loose ends."

"Organizing your life into nice tidy bundles?"

Lee dropped down beside her in the swing. "You could say that."

"So which bundle did you put me in?"

"Liza —"

"You shouldn't have taken Mr. Wilson from his guests."

Lee slipped an arm about her shoulders. "You're right. I'm sorry. I shouldn't have deserted you either. Forgive me?"

She wasn't finished. "And thanks for the advance warning about your parents."

He nodded. "Are you going to make me apologize all night?"

"I should. You keep pricking my stupid pride."

"Not stupid, my darling," he said, flashing her a loving smile. "That Carolina pride was my undoing. It's one of the things I love most about you. I was tying up loose ends so I could get on with the next phase of my life."

"What could possibly be so important?"

"This." Confused, Liza stared down at the family Bible he handed her.

Lee reached to open the leather cover. A gasp left her throat as Liza stared down at the names written on the matrimony page and the beautiful diamond solitaire looped on the ribbon bookmark. "Name the date and place. I'll be there. And God willing, one day we'll fill in our children's names."

Tears of joy ran unchecked down her cheeks.

"I know you're upset with me now, but I wanted everything to be taken care of before I asked you to be my wife. Uncle John and I have come to an agreement about the practice, so I can promise you we'll be close to your parents and the farm. And I know you were concerned about my commitment to God."

"I never should have judged you."

"Liza, I don't want anything to cloud your feelings for me, including doubt. That's why I waited to ask until after I completed my new-believer class. I now fully understand the step I've taken and embrace my faith openly."

"What about our differences, Lee? You've got law, and I've got the farm. How do we get past that?"

"Easier than if we throw our love away. We can have a family, Liza. Perhaps our son, or maybe daughter, will have the same passion for the land you and your father share. Just give us a chance."

"I want to — more than anything in the world."

"With God in our corner, we'll make it," Lee promised. His arms became her haven. "So how do I ask? Do you want a grand proposal like Kitty's? Me on bended knee in front of everyone?"

"No," she insisted, hugging him tighter. "Just us. Tell me you love me and ask me again. This time I'll be proud to say yes."

"And I'll be proud to have you as my wife. You're the second-best thing that ever happened to me, Sarah Elizabeth Stephens."

She knew his relationship with God held the number one slot, and Liza willingly accepted Lee's choice. "So are you going to ask?"

Lee untied the ring and knelt before her, taking her hand in his, "Will you do me the honor of becoming my wife?"

Thank You, Lord, she whispered softly. "Yes, my love. Yes."

The employees of Thorndike Press hope you have enjoyed this Large Print book. All our Thorndike and Wheeler Large Print titles are designed for easy reading, and all our books are made to last. Other Thorndike Press Large Print books are available at your library, through selected bookstores, or directly from us.

For information about titles, please call:
   (800) 223-1244

or visit our Web site at:
   www.gale.com/thorndike
   www.gale.com/wheeler

To share your comments, please write:
   Publisher
   Thorndike Press
   295 Kennedy Memorial Drive
   Waterville, ME 04901